The Cat Stalker's Sonnets

THE
CAT
STALKER'S
SONNETS

Marlene Mesot

Print layout and e-book conversion by
DLD Books Editing and Self-Publishing Services
www.dldbooks.com

ISBN: 978-1-7347393-0-5

4 Elements of Mystery Series

1. The Purging Fire
2. The Snowball Effect
3. Whirlwind of Fear
4. Terra Terror

www.marlsmenagerie.com/

Proverbs 15:13

A joyful heart makes a cheerful face,
But when the heart is sad, the spirit is broken.

Contents

1. See the Blind Cat 11

2. The Past Becomes Present 23

3. A Cat and Mouse Game 33

4. The Writing on the Wall 47

5. A Common Bond 65

6. Invitations 79

7. A Gift 87

8. The Costume Party 97

9. Mistaken Identity 113

10. Seeking Solace 121

11. Love Regained 133

12. Police Interrogation 141

13. See The Black Cat 147

14. Imagining 155

15. Picturesque 161

16. Double Trouble 171

17. It's About Truth 185

18. Chase the Cat 195

19. The Cat Stalker 207

20. The Cat Stalker's Sonnets 219

BONUS MATERIAL 229

1. See the Blind Cat

The sudden screech caused Lucas Hoffman to turn and retrace his steps toward the apartment that he had just recently left. The sound fleetingly reminded the veterinarian of a cantankerous tabby who had met her match, but Catrin Lein reminded him more of a soft kitten. However, now was not the time for reflection on the woman he had so recently met. Within seconds he was knocking on her door.

"Cathy, what's wrong?" He called to her. "It's Luke, Cathy."

The door opened to reveal a trembling female whose tear filled hazel eyes and quivering lips reminded Lucas of a stricken doe. She held her eyeglasses in one hand and had pressed the other to her mouth upon releasing the door knob.

Fearing that she might fall, Lucas instinctively grasped her trembling arms for support. "Cathy, what is it?"

Her voice shook as she managed to stammer, "...out on the fire escape...bedroom window...a, dead cat. There are no...no...eyes!"

Her companion led the woman to sit down in a high backed stuffed chair and then he left her to observe the scene for himself. When he returned moments later, he asked to use her phone to call the animal officer. She nodded slowly. Hearing the last words he spoke into the mouthpiece caused her to burst into sobs again. It wasn't the fact that the animal had been killed by someone breaking its neck, and there were no teeth marks so it must have been a human hand, but the fact that it had been pregnant. Cathy was crying not just for cats, but for all the babies that would never have a chance at life.

Her forehead came to rest on a smooth creamy silken shoulder. The gentle pressure of a hand on her head smoothing her honey brown hair and the palm on her back were meant to sooth and comfort. As Cathy breathed in the scent of aftershave, she suddenly realized that she was in the arms of a man who was practically a stranger.

"I know...I know." He was murmuring.

She moved, under his touch, to raise her face and look at his. The drooping mouth above a square chin made his face seem exaggeratedly long. She had an urge to put her glasses back on so that she could lose herself in those emerald colored eyes that seemed to be brimming with compassion at this moment. She turned to feel on the square end table beside the chair for her glasses. His arms still held her. As her hand reached out, she knocked a gray and white stuffed cat to the floor.

As if sudden awareness of his place dawned, the man withdrew his arms, stood quickly from his kneeling place on the floor in front of her and went to pick up the adornment.

"Lucas, I'm sorry." Cathy apologized when she had regained her composure at last.

"Perfectly understandable." He was smiling when he sat down at the corner of the couch angling the end table.

With her glasses intact, Cathy could see that this handsome man could easily hold any woman captive with such an alluring smile. She willed herself to concentrate on his words.

He was saying, "Don't worry, it will be taken care of."

She nodded, then, remembering her manners, she asked him, "Would you like some more coffee? I know we just went out for dinner, but, well..." She left the sentence unfinished. Cathy didn't want him to leave right now.

"Sure, why not?"

"Come into the kitchen while I make a pot." She offered.

Lucas rose to follow her. It was clear that she didn't want to be alone. He watched Cathy as she prepared the coffee for brewing. A slow easy smile parted his lips as he thought about his grandparent's farm where he had grown. The smell of perked coffee brewing always reminded him of home and his mother and grandmother chatting as they prepared meals together. His family had spent a lot of time around the kitchen table. With endless chores, mealtime became sharing time for all family members as his grandmother had expressed it. A soft sigh and a chair scraping brought his thoughts back to the present.

Cathy sat down across from him, rested both elbows on the edge of the table and leaned her chin in her hands. "What are you smiling at?" She asked him.

"Just thinking."

"Should I ask what about?"

He chuckled a little. "Don't worry. I was remembering the farm where I grew up. The smell of fresh coffee brewing makes me think of my family up state. Cozy little home feelin', you know."

But Cathy shook her head slowly and she was frowning.

"Cathy, what's wrong?" Lucas sat forward and dropped his smile.

She waved a hand in the air and then slid it back under her chin. "It's nothing. Not everybody had such a great childhood. But I don't think I should go into that. This is hardly starting our business relationship off on a casual footing."

Lucas winked one eye at her. "I'd rather we didn't."

"Didn't what?" She asked.

"Cathy, I know you said strictly business when you took me on as your client for your answering service, but I was hoping to change your mind on that tonight. That's partly why I asked you out to dinner. I'd like to get to know you better...personally."

Cathy drew in her breath as the coffee pot continued to gurgle. After their encounter in the living room she thought he knew her very well for a first date, especially one that was supposed to be a casual business outing. She touched a finger to the bow of her glasses, as if trying to make adjustment in order to see him better. How could this man be so open with his emotions, so honest, so captivating?

Realizing that she was staring, she got up to unplug the coffee pot which had suddenly become silent, too.

"Well, I suppose..." she stammered without looking at her male companion.

"Oh I hope I haven't offended you." Lucas exclaimed as a new thought struck him. "I can be a perfect gentleman, I assure you. It's just that you were so upset. I always comforted my younger sisters when they got hurt. I just didn't think. It was a natural reaction. I'm sorry. Is that what's bothering you? I mean, when I tried to comfort you...earlier?" He gestured toward the living room.

She was smiling when she brought their cups to the table. What a treat to find a man with such an old fashioned nature in this modern age, she thought. Most women would have been leading him toward the bedroom after such treatment and he was worried that he might have offended her with his demonstration of genuine concern and kindness. "No, not at all." Cathy corrected him. "Lucas, it's me, not you."

He shook his head and a wave of golden hair fell across his forehead enhancing his charm.

Cathy turned her back to go to the cupboard after a package of cookies. All her senses were warning her against emphatuation. She told herself to be careful. "Truth is, I haven't really dated much..." Cathy hoped her voice didn't sound as heavy to him as it did to herself. After the short pause she hastened to add, "lately." When she returned to the table with the plate of cookies he was grinning.

"Me neither." He said simply.

She looked from his face to the plate of cookies, then offered defensively, "No I don't bake home made stuff."

He laughed filling the room with momentary melody. "Now don't get defensive. I didn't say anything."

Cathy removed her glasses and set them on the table as the steam from her cup had clouded her vision. She was closely concentrating on sweetening her beverage.

His voice was soft when he spoke. "You look prettier without your glasses. Have you ever seen a deer?" He asked her.

"Not really. My vision is not very good without...Why do you ask?" She held his gaze when she raised her head.

"Just wondered. They are very timid and beautiful creatures."

"Animal lover, I see. I've never had any pets, but I've held cats belonging to other people I've visited." She admitted. "Some day I will have a real cat. Most apartments don't allow pets where I have lived."

He nodded. "When I was growing up I took in all the strays. I was sure I could doctor them all back to health. My mom knew I wanted to be a veterinarian even before I did. She used to tell me, 'Now, Luke, you can't save the whole animal world, you know. It's time you quit trying.'"

Cathy smiled. "But you didn't quit, huh?"

He shook his head and that soft golden wave settled down over his brow again. "Tell me about you, Cathy. It takes guts to venture out on your own to start a new business alone."

"Not much to tell." She wriggled in her chair. "I used to be house manager for a group home for developmentally disabled adults. After five years I decided it was time for a change, so I took my savings, got a loan and moved here to try something different."

"Tell me about your childhood?" He ventured.

"City kid. Foster care. The story is that my parents were killed in an auto accident while I was still in the hospital. I was a premature baby and so then I became a ward of the state. Now I'm just trying to survive like everyone else."

He nodded silently.

When the telephone rang, Catrin glanced at the kitchen clock. The oversized numbers told her it was quarter past eleven. "I'd better answer that." She rose and went into the living room. "Hello, Lein's Answering Line. May I help you?" Automatically she checked the answering machine to be sure it was recording the conversation.

Luke, who had been standing in the kitchen doorway, came to stand beside her as he saw her face pale noticeably. She drew in her breath, starting to speak, but was apparently interrupted. Her hand tightened on the receiver.

"Who?" She was finally able to expel the word but by then the phone had gone dead.

Cathy was grateful for the warmth of the hands now gently wrapped around her forearms, since she felt suddenly chilled. The sparkling brilliance of the eyes she was now holding reminded her of jewels she had seen in store glass casings. There seemed to be a light of inner strength in them that she could not fathom. Cathy longed to linger in the security of his touch. Forcing herself to look away, she touched a button on the machine in order to rewind, then replay the message.

After the beep the following lines were grated out in a slow deep male voice like a record being played at too slow a speed:

See the blind cat.
You can't escape that.
First to mate—
A fatal mistake.

Ne're to wed,
For now she is dead.

Click. The phone went dead cutting off Cathy's response even before she could utter it.

"Prank caller?" Her voice was a quivering whisper and her eyes sought his questioningly.

"Come sit down." She offered no protest when his arms guided her to the couch and he sat down close to her. She looked down as his grip loosened and his hands began to slip away. Without thinking she reached out to grasp them again. She barely heard his soft murmur.

"Cold hands, warm heart."

"Oh, Luke," she kept looking at their hands, "I keep thinking about that poor cat." Her grip tightened slightly. When she looked up he was nodding. His mouth was drawn together in a grim line. Cathy longed to feel the comfort of his embrace, to lose herself in his emerald green eyes, but she fought the urge with concentrated effort. She had to force herself to hear what he was saying.

"Cathy, it's getting late and I should be going...but you don't look like you're all right. You need something to take your mind off..." He shrugged his shoulders. Then he asked, "Do you enjoy reading?"

"Reading?" She echoed.

"Ya. When I can't sleep I read Psalm 119."

"You mean in the Bible?" She fervently hoped her new found companion wasn't one of those religious fanatics. "I'm more into classical literature." She responded. She had turned away hoping her face did not reveal her disappointment.

"Just a suggestion." He stood. "Cathy, if you need anything, anytime, you can call me. You have my private phone number."

She rose to her full five foot three inch height. The top of her head barely reached his chin. "Really? That is a comfort to me, Luke. Thank you. I mean it."

Her heart leaped involuntarily when his lips brushed a brief kiss to her forehead. So fleeting was the gesture that she barely felt their touch.

"Sweet dreams, Luke." She said to his back at the door,

surprising herself with the bold statement. When he turned she had regained a smile and her eyes shone clear.

The grin he gave to her made his face look youthful. "You remind me of one of my sisters. Good night, Cathy."

The telephone ringing awakened Catrin the next morning. She sat upright in bed startled by the abrupt sound. Half way through the third ring the noise ceased. She lay back down against the pillow with a sigh. The answering machine was a wonderful addition to life, she decided, even if it was her business. Her right hand groped for the square clock on her nightstand table. Holding it close to her eyes, she realized that the work day had already begun. It was several minutes past eight. She replaced the clock and stretched under her covers. She did not know how long she had lain in bed before sleep had claimed her the previous night. When the phone shrilled again, Cathy promptly picked up the extension which also sat on her nightstand. "Lein's Answering Line, good morning." She announced in a synonymously cheerful tone.

"Well it's about time I got a person instead of a machine!" The voice boomed almost painfully in her ear. "I am a physician whom people depend upon. If I am going to use an answering service for backup, I expect it to be alive and not a machine!"

"Yes, doctor, I know. But, if I had been, say, in the bathroom, I never would have gotten this call without the machine. In that case, if you had left a name and number, I could have called right back. Sometimes the machine can be an advantage you see?"

The raspy sound of throat clearing was not pleasing to her ear. "Well, at any rate, I'm Paul Davis, DDS." He paused.

Taking her cue Cathy replied. "Yes, you are the dentist. Would you like to discuss my hours and fees? I am available twenty–four hours a day, machine included." The latter was spoken in a gentler tone of voice.

"I'd like to hear about your credentials first."

"Of course." Cathy responded pleasantly. After she had explained, the dentist finally agreed to enlist her services on a trial basis. After hanging up the phone Cathy got up to go into the bathroom to take her shower. When she turned the faucet a yawning groan erupted to startle her ears but no water ran forth. She sighed and turned the faucet again. The noise repeated itself.

"Great. Air in the line." She muttered. Then, hearing the telephone beckon, she went to answer it. To her delight she acquired another customer. Maybe this will work out after all she told herself gaining confidence in her venture. Next she went to the kitchen to get the number for the building manager so she could report her water problem. She dressed hurriedly. Not long after a knock sounded at her door, apartment number 229.

"Morning ma'am." The low key voice belonged to a man not much taller than herself who had darker brown hair, with a touch of gray, closely cropped. He also wore glasses. "Something wrong?"

Realizing she was staring, Cathy stepped aside to allow him to enter the apartment. "For a moment I thought you looked...familiar." Cathy stammered. "You are the building manager I assume?"

He nodded his head briefly. "Yes, ma'am. Name's Fr...Frazer, Max Frazer. Call me Max. And you're Catrin Lein." He stated. At her gaping mouth stare he hastened to add, "I saw your name in the recently up dated tenants registry. What seems to be the problem?"

"Air in the pipe for the bathroom I think. This way."

Cathy looked into his face again touching the bridge of her glasses with her finger before leading the way to the trouble.

2. The Past Becomes Present

Several days later, in mid afternoon, Cathy darted to the phone before the answering machine could pick up after the third ring. She found herself hoping it might be the handsome animal doctor Lucas Hoffman. She answered cheerfully. "Lein's Answering Line."

She just heard breathing. Cathy's heart began to pound faster."Hello. I know someone is there. Answer me!" She demanded.

"Ca...Cat?"

Catrin pulled in her breath sharply. She hadn't been called that since she worked with...Her mind scrambled to search and recall. She then remembered her fondness for one of her clients in particular from the residential group home where she had previously worked. But it couldn't be her. How could she find me here? Cathy had to answer. No time to reminisce now. Eagerly now she responded. "Jess, is that you?"

"Hi, Cat. It is, it is, I'm Jess Reed. Miss Shelton helped me to find you. I am so glad I find you, Cat. Guess what?"

"Jess, where are you calling from?"

"Guess what, Cat?" Jess repeated.

"What, Jess." Cathy knew she needed to play along to get her friend to explain.

"I got a re–partment by you. Meet me in the wash room, you know, where you wash your clothes, what is it called?"

"The laundry room?" Cathy suggested.

"Yes, right now. Can you meet me there right now?"

"Jess, slow down." Cathy spoke slowly. She knew that re–partment meant apartment. Surely Jessica Reed wasn't in this very building, unless her social worker, Miss Nancy Shelton, had helped her arrange to move to Manchester, New Hampshire?

"You and me are in the same place, see?" Frustration began to edge the younger woman's voice. "Please, Cat, right now, you gotta come."

"Is Miss Shelton there with you now?" Cathy asked.

"No. How could she do that?" Jess sounded as if this was a most absurd statement to make. "Miss Shelton is in Hanover, New Hampshire. You know that."

"Okay, Jess. I will meet you in the laundry room in a few minutes. Do you know where it is?"

"Yes." The line clicked dead.

Cathy leaned forward toward the mirror, which hung above her bureau, to check her make up and comb her hair. She smiled wryly to herself. She knew it wouldn't make any difference to Jess, because her sight was worse than Cathy's. They were both legally blind, although Cathy was just barely borderline of the definition. Even so, it would be a delight to see her witty friend again. Watch it, her conscience warned. Let the cat out of the bag and it's trouble. You don't want to get hurt again, remember? No attachments. She sighed and tossed her comb gently to the bureau top. Automatically she went to the answering machine to check to be sure it was in record mode with plenty of tape. Then she picked up her purse from her bedside stand and walked out locking her apartment door as she left.

When Cathy arrived there was no mistaking the solitary occupant of the laundry room. Even without the short red hair and bangs fashioned in a boyish cut, Cathy would have recognized the taller, slender body of Jessica Reed. Only the black and blue circles under her eyes from excessive rubbing detracted from this younger woman's physical beauty. Forgetting all her previous guards against showing emotion, Cathy stepped toward the other female with arms outstretched.

"Jess, it's so good to see you."

They embraced with mutual affection. Jess, for she hated to be called by her full given name, remembered Cathy's patience and encouragement with her personal problems when they were at the group home. Cathy felt the slimmer body begin to tremble in her arms.

"Oh, Jess, don't cry." Cathy heard her own voice quivering. Once they had finally gotten control of their emotions, Cathy asked her first question. She tried not to overwhelm her friend with more than one at a time. "Did you come here by yourself?"

"No. Miss Shelton helped me to find a place and Jim Ashton and some of the strong guys helped us move my things here."

Cathy's smile quivered a little at the mention of Jim's name. She had gotten to know him, also a resident staff member at the group home, almost too well.

As if reading her thoughts Jess asked, "Have you gotten a new boyfriend yet, Cat?" Unknowingly, Jess had an uncanny way of getting right to the point.

"I haven't been here very long, Jess. Although, I have met a rather handsome man recently." Cathy smiled at Jess'es delighted giggle. Then she added, "I hope he calls me again."

"They just went back to Hanover yesterday night." Jess was saying. "Miss Shelton helped me find your phone number and she wrote it big for me so I could see it. Come on I'll show you my re–partment." Jess took Cathy's hand to lead Cathy to her new place of residence.

"Can you help me get a job, Cat? Miss Shelton said you got a business. Can I work with you, huh, Cat?"

"Wait, Jess, not so fast." Cathy scarcely took in all the information and its implications. "I am just starting out on my own too, in a way. I work alone." The last was said slowly and thoughtfully. "Jess, how are you going to manage your own money?"

"Miss Shelton will and she will give me some every week. I get disability money every month, but I want to work too, like you do, Cat."

The one bedroom apartment looked huge with its sparse furnishings. A couch, one easy chair and a coffee table dotted the living room. A card table and four folding chairs leaned against the wall opposite the sink in the kitchen. One twin bed and a bureau stood stalwartly in the single bedroom. Window shades lay bare with no curtains to adorn them.

"What's the ;matter, Cat? Don't you like it? I do."

Cathy sighed and then answered carefully. "It is a fine start, Jess. Maybe I could help you buy some curtains and lamps, you know, as a house warming gift. How about it?"

"Okay. You and me can go shopping, huh Cat?"

Cathy's honey colored hair bounced as she nodded. Then, without even thinking about it, she asked, "So, Jim knows where you, where we, live now right?"

Jess nodded. "Everybody knows where you moved to now because I moved here too." Jess said the words proudly.

Cathy nodded and sat down on the vinyl printed couch cushion. She refused to let her mind dwell on that piece of news. Cathy began to look in her purse for paper and pen. She always carried a small notebook just in case she met prospective clients or needed to jot down something important. "Give me your phone number, Jess."

A puzzled look crossed the other woman's face. "Oh, I don't know it."

"That's okay, Jess. It is probably written somewhere on your phone. Where is it?"

"It's on the kitchen counter. You think so? I hope it is." Jess led the way into the next room. Upon examination of the item, Cathy found the number and copied it down. She peeled another piece of paper from her notebook to print her friend's name and phone number for her to have also. "Put this under the phone so you will have it." She handed the paper to her friend. Automatically Cathy went to the refrigerator to make sure that Jess had food to eat. She knew that the woman was capable of cooking her own meals. Jess used to help her at the group home when Cathy had staff duty.

Before going back to her own affairs, Cathy took the time to explain and show her friend how to find her own apartment, which was just down the hall. After explaining about her answering machine, Cathy left her friend to return to her own apartment in order to check for messages in her absence.

While the coffee pot gurgled happily, Cathy sat down to listen to the recording. To her dismay there were several beeps and clicks without any messages. She wished that people wouldn't just hang up the phone without at least leaving their names. Then, following a beep, there was a long pause before a sound became audible, still rising in intensity. Startled, Cathy sat straight, upright in her chair, listening intently. It was heavy breathing. It became louder. Cathy stopped the machine. Then sounds behind her made her jump. She stood and finally realized that it was the coffee pot babbling at her. Why a prank call on an answering machine, she wondered. Once silenced, she started to pour the coffee, but had to put the pot down to steady her shaking hand. Then she succeeded in pouring. With the hot brew before her, Cathy again sat down to face the recording machine. She switched on the play button and the loud, heavy breathing continued until the click several breaths later. The next beep and then...

"Call me at the office when you get in, would ya, Cathy? It's Luke." He repeated the number.

A familiar voice! In her haste Cathy almost whisked her coffee cup to the floor. She stopped the machine and punched the push buttons on her phone quickly. A wide eyed stare at the large numbers on her wall clock indicated it was almost time for the veterinarian office to close.

"Doctor Hoffman here."

The soft but clear tones were so welcome to her ear that she almost began to cry. Cathy choked and then coughed.

"Hello?" A slight impatience edged his voice.

"Luke...I...I'm so glad you answered." Cathy stammered and then paused to gather her breath. Finally she added, "I got a prank call and it, it sort of scared me, a little. I just now got your message to call you back. How...how are you?"

"Well, I was going to ask you out to dinner again. But, if you'd rather, I could just come over? I am leaving the office now. Are you all right?"

"Yes." This was said with a little too much emphasis. "Luke, I could make dinner for us here." The words spilled out before she had time to even think about what she was saying. "I mean, I really shouldn't be going out if I am on call, you know."

"Good point. That's fine. Mind if I come early?"

Again she answered without forethought and it was too eager. "Right away if you like."

"Great. I'll see you soon."

Their conversation ended.

Cathy hung up the receiver and stood for a moment as if replaying the conversation over in her mind. What did I do? Her mind finally registered what she had offered. The overwhelming desire to talk to someone—anyone—was now replaced by a growing apprehension. After all, this would be only their second date, so to speak. She had never invited Jim into her apartment until they had been dating for several weeks and look what he had tried to do. She put her hands to her mouth to suppress the sound. Should she invite Jess too? No. She didn't know how this animal lover would react to someone with special needs. Some people didn't accept those conditions as readily as she did. Practically speaking she was visually handicapped herself. It was not something that she readily admitted, but it was true enough. Then her rambling mind took another turn. Food! What to eat? She turned to stare at her cupboards for a moment. Think, Catrin. Think clearly. Her mind chided her. As she reached for her luke warm coffee the phone rang again.

When he arrived, Cathy greeted Lucas at the door with a

cheerful smile. "One of your patients called." She quickly told him.

He returned it then spoke pleasantly. "Now, that's much better. All right, don't tell me, I think it was Mrs. Grayson?"

Cathy nodded, then gestured. "Come into the kitchen. I hope you don't mind spaghetti with store bought sauce."

He chuckled agreeably.

"Mrs. Grayson is worried about her Tabatha. She wanted you to know that her cat had morning sickness this afternoon and she wondered if it was a result of being examined today. She thinks that her cat might be still nervous." Cathy turned to look at him then. "Really, Luke. It's just an animal."

"Oh no," he replied, "Tabatha is Mrs. Grayson's baby. They have no children, you see, so that cat gets better treatment than some people I know, I dare say. Sounds like everything is normal, but I'll call her just for reassurance, if you don't mind, boss?" He grinned at her.

Cathy repeated the expletive rather than expressing it. "Ha, I work for you. Remember? Sure, go ahead and call her."

Still smiling, he gently pushed the buttons on the phone upon retrieving the number from her answering machine. It was not long before he spoke soothingly. "Dr. Hoffman here, Mrs. Grayson." A moment later he was explaining that it was perfectly normal for Tabatha to have morning sickness. It was merely a coincidence that it began the same day as her examination. Yes, he was sure. "You're welcome, Mrs. Grayson. If nothing else comes up, we'll see you and Tabatha next month." Then he was re–explaining how to drop the measure of liquid vitamin into her food every morning. Following a short pause, he repeated his salutation, then said good–bye and hung up the receiver.

"I hope all your patients aren't that eccentric." Cathy observed when he had sat down at the table with her. "It was nice of you to call, but that wasn't really an emergency."

"Doesn't have to be." He replied simply. Luke bowed his head momentarily , then began to eat.

The coffee pot sputtered while they ate their meal.

"So, how's business?" He asked her congenially.

"I have a few more clients now." She told him. Then remembering she added, "Oh, I saw an old friend today. You remember I told you I used to work as house manager for a group home for developmentally disabled adults in Hanover?"

He nodded while eating.

"Well, one of the residents, Jessica Reed, moved here and got an apartment by herself. I know her quite well."

"Mm. That's great."

"Really?" Cathy sounded surprised.

"Sure. I'm all for people trying to better themselves, no matter what the circumstances. Some people who claim to be mentally slow have more sense than some of those who say they are normal. Some animals are quick to learn and others just never catch on. It's the same with people."

Cathy sighed then asked him, "Do you always compare people to animals, Luke?"

"Most times." He replied readily.

She got up to fill their coffee cups. Once she had sat down again she stirred her coffee then asked him, "What kind of animal am I?"

There was something warm and touching in his green eyes as they gazed steadily upon her face. He replied quietly. "A doe, my dear." His seriously tender look tugged at her heart as their gazes held for a long serene moment.

3. A Cat and Mouse Game

Since her hurriedly prepared dinner with the kind and captivating animal doctor, Cathy's spirits glided happily along a smooth course. She had forgotten about the obscene prank call and, after all, she was getting new customers all the time. She had promised Jess a shopping trip and was now preparing to go meet her friend for the event.

"Well, it's about time you got here." Jess exclaimed when Cathy had arrived. But there was a curved smile to her lips indicating a hint of laughter after the reprimand.

Cathy nodded and they started toward the front door of the apartment building. Outside on the large cement landing Cathy recognized the man who had fixed her faucets and spoke congenially to him. "Hello, Mr. Frazer."

The man looked up from his sweeping, nodded shortly, then looked down again.

Cathy continued speaking. "This is my friend Jess Reed. She's—"

The man grunted his interruption. "New tenant. I know. Excuse me." He had finished sweeping and pushed past them to go inside without looking up.

"Boy," Jess exclaimed, "I guess he don't like us much."

Cathy replied as they walked slowly down the steps. "Oh, I wouldn't say that. He doesn't know us yet. He is the building manager and maintenance man so he takes care of the office and the grounds."

"Oh. I know, like the men do at the day care place in Hanover. He kinda reminds me of that guy, oh, you know who I mean, don't you, Cat?"

Cathy nodded. "You mean the grounds keeper at the recreation center where the staff used to take you and the others?"

Jess agreed. "Ya. He was only there a short time. Let me think." After a short pause Jess recalled the name. "His name was Frank Morrow. He used to tell me not to ask so many questions. This man that we just met, Mr. Frazer, he reminds me of that man, Frank Morrow, because of how he walks and makes noise with his feet."

Cathy smiled and then remarked. "Jess, I don't know how you do it. You never forget a name. Sometimes I think you are smarter than you think you are."

Her friend giggled happily.

Cathy had only met Frank Morrow briefly for his stay as grounds keeper couldn't have been more than a couple of months at most. Jess remembered him. Cathy would be willing to bet that Jess could recall everyone she had ever met in her life. Then Cathy said impulsively, "Jess, how would you like to meet my new friend Luke after we go shopping? Maybe we could stop by his office later?"

"Sure. I would love to meet your new boyfriend."

"Oh, please don't say that in front of him, okay, Jess?"

Jess giggled.

Armed with their bags, Cathy and Jess walked into the

veterinarian's office shortly before closing time that afternoon. There were still two patients waiting, Cathy observed, as she saw two people sitting patiently in chairs. One held a small dog on her lap. The other was a man holding a leash that was attached to a police dog, Cathy guessed, because the man was wearing a policeman's uniform. Before Cathy fully comprehended what was happening, Jess had deposited her bags on the floor and was stepping toward the white bundle in the small feminine lap.

"Oh, what a cute thing." Jess approached her with hand outstretched in order to pet the terrier.

The white dog began to yip in high pitched yelps as slim arms came around to enclose it protectively. The pet owner leveled a glowering stare at the young red head. As the yipping continued, the police dog began to bark in deep, nonstop rhythm. Cathy was reminded of a military march, disciplined and in perfect precision timing.

"What's this?" A female voice snapped.

The barking from both animals abruptly ceased.

Cathy, who had hastily pulled Jess aside to avoid disaster, turned to observe a beautiful young blonde woman who was not much taller than herself. Her deep blue eyes were wide and staring at Cathy's friend.

The woman's voice was stern as she spoke further. "I'm afraid you'll have to step outside, Miss. You are disturbing our patients."

Cathy spoke up quickly. "I'm sorry, we didn't mean to. I'm Cathy Lein, Dr. Hoffman's answering service, and this is my friend Jess Reed. We would like to see the doctor when he is through, I mean, before he leaves, please."

"Is there some business? Do you have an appointment?"

The sunny blonde head lifted slightly.

Cathy shook her head. "No, it's a personal visit."

"Well, I'll see if he has the time. Wait here and be quiet." The blonde in the white lab coat turned to go back into the examining room.

Once they were seated, Jess asked quietly, "Cat, what did I do? I just wanted to pet the little dog."

"I know, but that dog didn't know you. The owner didn't know that you were just trying to be friendly. Don't worry about it, Jess." Cathy tried to reassure her friend.

"That lady wasn't very nice to us."

"Lady?" Cathy murmured to herself, then she said more audibly, "She must be his assistant."

Finally silence prevailed. The man kept looking at his watch, Cathy noticed, while the older woman petted and cuddled her bundle.

Several minutes later the blonde in the lab coat appeared again and announced, "Whitey Shea, you may go in now."

"Wait, Miss Becker." The man barked in a commanding voice.

The slender hand resting briefly on his shoulder reminded Cathy of an add for artificial nails. "You're next, Mr. Pierceson." Then she disappeared again behind the door.

"Whitey?" Jess asked. "That woman had gray hair."

"It is probably the dog's first name and the owner's last name put together." Cathy surmised.

"Oh." Jess nodded.

Several minutes following Mr. Pierceson's departure with Rinny, his shepherd, Luke Hoffman poked his head around the door to peer into the waiting room. "All clear?" He asked no one in particular. Spotting Cathy he widened the door to step out. He too wore a white lab coat, but his hung open revealing his blue shirt and brown trousers. His smile was reflected in his pleasant voice when he spoke. "Cathy, I didn't know you were here." He approached her with hand outstretched in greeting.

"But..."

The blonde interrupted Cathy's query. "I was going to tell you, Luke, after all your patients had left. I know how important your patients are to you, Luke, and you were so busy this afternoon."

"Okay, Lucy." He turned his head momentarily to glance at his petite assistant. "Lucy Becker, my office assistant, meet Cathy Lein, my new answering service owner."

Cathy squeezed his warm fingers and smiled up at him.

"Well, then, if you are going to be busy, Luke, I guess I'll be going now." The blonde shot Cathy a scowl.

"See ya tomorrow, Lucy." He did not take his gaze away from Cathy.

"What's the matter with her?" Jess asked.

"Oh." Cathy had forgotten to introduce her friend. "Luke, this is my friend Jess Reed. I told you about her."

Luke finally released Cathy's hand to extend his to the other woman. "Hello, Jess. I am Luke Hoffman. I work with Cathy."

"Hi." Jess said and smiled. Then she asked him, "Why do you call her Cathy?"

"What?" Luke was bewildered by this question.

"I always call her Cat." Jess explained briefly.

The veterinarian smiled broadly.

"Either way is fine." Cathy assured them. "Catrin is so formal sounding."

Luke nodded approvingly. "Cat, I like it. Well, I see you two have been shopping."

Cathy explained. "Yes, it is for Jess'es new apartment. She now lives in the same building with me."

Jess remarked. "We must have walked all over town. It is nice in here with the cool air."

Luke nodded then turned to Cathy again. "May I offer you ladies a ride home?"

Cathy answered quickly. "Oh, we don't want to impose."

"My pleasure."

His reply was so tender and genuine Cathy thought.

Jess accepted quickly before Cathy could change his mind. "Thank you, Luke. Would you like to see my place?"

He nodded and held the door for them. Since he was the last one to leave, he made sure that all was secure before he too went outside, locked the main entrance and set the security alarm. There he joined the two women in the warm summer afternoon sunshine.

Later, when the threesome had entered Cathy's apartment with their pizza, the phone was ringing. Cathy hurried to interrupt the machine and answer the call. "Lein's Answering Line. May I help you?"

Even Luke and Jess could hear the voice that boomed out at her although they could not distinguish the words. Then Cathy spoke.

"I'm sorry Dr. Davis. Yes, I know it is past your closing time. I just returned from important errands. Yes, I do realize that clients, uh, patients could be trying to...Yes, that's why I have the machine, in case I can't get to the phone immediately. I check it often, as soon as I can after being absent...or busy...No, it won't happen again. I can assure you...No, I have no calls for you at this time. Yes, I will be here all evening. That will be fine. Good–bye, Dr. Davis."

Jess immediately commented. "Boy, you can't call your time your own. Cat, do you have something to drink?"

Cathy touched a finger to the bridge of her glasses to push them up. "Oh, yes, just a minute. I'll get some soft drinks to go with the pizza."

"I'll help you carry them." Luke offered and followed her into the kitchen. He closed the kitchen door behind them then came to put his hands on her shoulders. "Slow down and relax a minute, Cathy." His voice was soothing. His hands gently pushed her down into a chair and then began massaging her tense shoulders. Then he asked her, "Want to talk about the phone call?"

"Phone call?" She echoed. Her mind was concentrating on what her body was feeling.

He reminded her. "Dr. Davis, the guy who just chewed you out for getting home late and not being here when he called to check in."

"Oh." It was more of a sigh than a response on her part. She wondered how she might fare as a piece of his pottery as the loss of tension left her feeling weak and pliable under his strong, tender touch. Without thinking about it she was saying, "That feels wonderful. Thank you, Luke."

He chuckled and gave her shoulders a gentle squeeze before letting go. Then he offered, "I'll get some ice."

"Ice?" She echoed again.

"For our drinks." He turned to go to the freezer.

"Of course." Cathy then stood and went to the cupboard hoping to hide her blush. She reached up and took out three tall glasses and set them down on the counter.

"Jess couldn't eat a whole pizza by herself could she?" Luke jested.

"I don't think so." Cathy said as she poured the liquid.

Once the glasses were filled Luke offered to carry the tray for her. They left the kitchen. Luke set the tray down on the coffee table in the living room and opened the pizza box to serve the ladies.

Jess exclaimed, "Goodness, what took you so long? I thought you went to the store to get it."

"We had to wait for the fizz." Cathy muttered.

Luke added. "We were just talking, Jess." When he took his own pizza he sat on the couch next to Cathy.

"Oh." Jess answered him.

They ate in silence for a time. Cathy was glad she had remembered to bring an ample supply of napkins on her way out of the kitchen. Finally Luke spoke.

"Cathy, I have been wanting to ask you, that is, invite you to a meeting. Perhaps Jess would like to come too?"

"What kind of meeting?" Cathy asked.

"We have a small group get together where we sing and talk and study the Bible."

Cathy looked up at him. "You want me to go to a Bible study?"

His lips curved into a smile but it quivered slightly. "It isn't that bad." He commented judging from her surprised expression. "It is fun really. We are all friendly people. You might like it after you get to know us."

"That sounds nice."

"Jess." Cathy exclaimed.

Jess continued. "Miss Shelton told us about Jesus being our Savior. Only I can't read the Bible, Luke."

Cathy saw the warmth glowing in his emerald eyes as Luke turned to smile across at Jess. "That's all right, Jess. God loves you just the way you are."

"I know."

It was said with such honesty, such meek shyness that Luke found himself admiring Cathy's fiery tempered friend.

His handsome features turned and those sparkling jewels were again giving Cathy their full attention. Willing herself to restrain her emotions, Cathy fought back. She turned to face him and asked, "Are you trying to convert me, Luke? Is this your game?"

His head shook resolutely. "No of course not, Cathy. I enjoy your company and I just wanted to share what I enjoy with you also."

There was such a sincere tone to his statement and look of honesty to his face. Still, Cathy's conscience warned her. Was he using a line on her for ulterior motives? Following a short silence she asked him, "Does Lucy Becker go to your meetings?"

Again his head shook. Then he told her. "She has made it very clear that she is definitely not interested. Won't you at least come to one gathering with an open mind? If you don't like it, I won't ask you again, okay?"

It was Jess who commented first. "That sounds fair, Cat. Come on, go at least once, with me? I want to see what it is like. Please?"

Cathy asked, "When is it?"

"It'll be next Thursday evening at seven o'clock. It usually runs until about nine."

Cathy was thoughtful. "Hmm. Dr. Davis has Thursday nights off. Another dentist covers for him so he probably won't be checking his service that evening. "I guess so, one time." She agreed.

Luke did not try to suppress his excitement. "You won't

regret it." After setting down his pizza and napkin on the coffee table, he turned to give the woman beside him. He put his arms around Cathy giving her a tight squeeze and a brief touch with his spicy lips against her forehead. "Thanks." He murmured. Then he released her as quickly as he had hugged her.

Just when she thought she had him figured out, Cathy did not know what to think now. She did not welcome the confusion and ferocity of emotion that pelted her when this man was near. It had not been like this when Jim had hugged her. She had always been in control of her feelings. To think that she had almost abandoned her control. How thankful she was now that she had not let her trust betray her. Unconsciously she edged closer to the arm of the couch so she wouldn't feel the touch of his thigh against hers. His closeness was overwhelming to her emotions.

As if reading her thoughts Jess asked, "What's the matter, Cat?"

She responded quickly. "Nothing."

When Luke spoke his tone was soft and gentle. "You look bewildered, Cat. Don't worry. You will have a good time, I know it."

When she heard his voice using her pet name it tugged at her heart. Her doe like gaze locked with his, seemingly drawing confidence and reassurance from him. When she heard Jess ask who was going to eat the last piece of pizza, Cathy forced herself to look away from her captor. She smiled in spite of her doubts and gestured for her friend to take it and eat.

Later, when Luke rose to leave, he offered to walk Jess to her own apartment. He had again expressed his joy at Cathy's decision and then left with Jess.

The excuse was perfect. Cathy had lain awake that night

after Luke had brought her and Jess home and gotten them pizza. Now she entered his office alone, with confidence. She really hadn't wanted to go to his Bible study meeting anyway. Jess would be disappointed, but it couldn't be helped, she told herself. Cathy began to walk past the receptionist toward the waiting area.

"May I help you, uh, Miss Lein, isn't it?"

So intent was she on her own thoughts, Cathy didn't realize she had been spoken to until she heard her name mentioned. Turning back toward the pleasant faced woman Cathy replied. "Yes, that's right, but please call me Cathy. I just need to talk to Dr. Hoffman briefly when he is through. I can wait, thank you."

The young woman nodded. "I'll let him know you are here, Cathy."

Cathy went to sit beside a middle aged woman holding a black cat on her lap. Her carrying crate sat in front of her.

Several minutes passed before the blonde in the lab coat opened the examination room door and stepped out. "Midnight Caldwell." She announced.

As she had expected, the woman seated next to Cathy rose with her pet.

Noticing Cathy, the blonde stepped toward her as the woman passed with her pet. Her voice was hostile toward Cathy.

"What are you doing here? I don't see an animal, Miss Lein. This is a vet's office."

Cathy nodded hoping this woman didn't have a pet either, four legged anyway. Aloud she answered her. "I just need to speak to the doctor a moment when he is through. It won't take long."

Lucy muttered her words but Cathy heard them. "Better not."

Mrs. Caldwell was walking out of the office door when Lucas stepped out into the waiting room. "Hi, Cathy, what can I do for you?" Then he smiled broadly.

Before Cathy had a chance to answer, Lucy came up behind him and spoke quickly. "Now, Luke, you promised to take me to dinner tonight. Don't forget." She hastily reminded him.

Then Cathy explained. "This won't take long, Luke." She assured him. "I just wanted to let you know that I can't come to your group meeting after all."

She saw the disappointment on his face. "Why, Cathy? I was really hoping that you would."

"Well, I thought about it, and I really shouldn't leave the phone for that long a time at night. You know, my business is just getting started."

Lucy backed her up. "You know she's right."

He nodded slowly. After a thoughtful pause he spoke. "Well then, how about this? Why don't we meet at your apartment. We usually take turns meeting at each other's place anyway. That is, if you don't mind that? You wouldn't want to disappoint Jess, would you?" His voice sounded hopeful.

"Luke, I don't know them."

"Tell you what. If you'll have coffee, we will bring the desserts."

If only his eyes weren't so pleadingly persuasive...

"Please, Cat? It would mean a lot to me." Luke spoke warmly, successfully imitating Jess.

"I guess so." Captivated by his demeanor the words had slipped without a thought or protest.

"Gee, Luke, that's quite an offer. Will you take me?"

His attention turned toward his assistant. "But, I thought you weren't interested, Lucy."

She stepped closer to the tall man and put her hand on his arm while smiling sweetly up into his face. Her hand tugged his arm urging him to lean down toward her. Then she put her lips close to his ear to whisper. "I really like dessert."

"Cathy?" Luke asked politely.

Cathy shrugged her shoulders. Not wanting to appear the heavy, Cathy agreed and forced herself to smile.

Delight sang genuinely in the man's voice. "That's wonderful! Both my girls are going! I am so pleased. Cathy, would you like a ride home? I'm sure Lucy won't mind."

Cathy shook her head quickly. She didn't need to continue playing a cat and mouse game with this opponent. She really wasn't planning to be in the competition anyway.

"Bye." Lucy again put her hand on the man's arm and turned to tug him toward the inner office. "Let's go, doctor. I'm getting hungry."

Cathy quickened her pace as she walked through the city to her apartment building. She did not want to leave her answering machine to manage for her for too long. She reminded herself that she must be more prompt about being home before five o'clock, the usual time of most business closings that she had to be concerned with. She sighed as she tried to erase the petite image of Lucy Becker from her mind. The young model–like assistant clearly had designs on her boss. And what about the handsome doctor, she reflected in her thoughts. Was his attention to her just that of friendship or could there be more in those emerald eyes? She felt her lips curve in an easy smile at the thought of him.

Instead of going through the park, she turned down a narrow alleyway desiring to take a short cut to her apartment building to save time. It should be safe enough in the still daylight. Upon hearing footsteps behind her, Cathy turned to glance over her shoulder. She caught her breath as a dark sleek figure disappeared behind a doorway. She noticed the person was dressed all in black, maybe wearing exercise clothing, she wondered. Thinking nothing of the brief incident, she continued on her way.

Finally turning a corner, she almost squealed with fright. Just for an instant, she saw the image of a black cat like person standing in front of her on two legs. Cathy looked around to see if anyone else was present. When she turned back to look ahead again, it was gone. She stood still for several moments not knowing exactly what to do. Bewildered, Cathy removed her glasses to stare at them as if disbelieving that no one had painted a picture of a black cat person on them to deceive her. Again she looked behind and in front of her. She knew she had seen something. Cathy was beginning to feel that she was the unfortunate victim of a cat and mouse game. She didn't like feeling small as a mouse. Replacing her glasses, Cathy sprinted for home.

4. The Writing on the Wall

"Really, Luke, you didn't have to go and do that." Cathy scolded him as she pointed to the notice on the public bulletin board beside the manager's office in her apartment building. "You didn't have to advertise the fact. You said just a few people."

"I'm sorry, Cathy. I just thought it might be a nice way for you to meet more of your neighbors and you could also advertise your new business."

Again she pointed to the bulletin board and her small business card that was hanging inconspicuously there.

Luke shook his head. "The personal touch makes a world of difference."

"Oh?" She wondered what situations he had applied this experience to.

"Sure does." He said simply.

Hearing a scuffling noise behind them, they both turned to see a man in a blue collar shirt standing behind them. "Trouble, ma'am?" He asked.

Cathy shook her head and then introduced Luke to the building supervisor, Max Frazer.

"Are you here much?" Luke asked in his get to the point manner.

Max nodded. "Every day from eight until two and I live in the building as well." He turned his blue eyes upon the object of their discussion. "Bible study at your place? Sounds interesting, Miss Lein."

"Sure, you're welcome to come, Mr. Frazer." What else could she do.

"Thanks. But please make it Max since we're neighbors after all, ma'am."

"My friend Jess will be there too. You met her the other day."

The shorter man nodded briefly.

Luke asked him, "Do you read the Bible, Max?"

"Nah. I like poetry. I'm a people watcher though." Max folded his arms across his chest and leaned to one side as if favoring the other.

Luke's smile ignited a warmth inside Cathy. This animal lover liked people too. When his hand closed around her forearm, her heart forgot itself for a moment.

"Cathy, we'd better be going if I'm going to have time to take you to lunch." Luke reminded.

Max walked away with a noticeable lag to one leg.

As Luke held the car door for her Cathy commented, "Strange man."

He closed the door and went around to duck into the driver's side. He was smiling and his voice was light hearted when he spoke. "I hope you don't mean me?"

She chuckled slightly and reassured him. "No, I mean Max, the maintenance man. He seems to appear out of nowhere and, sometimes, he doesn't even look at you when he speaks, if he speaks." She shrugged her shoulders. "He makes me uneasy sometimes."

"Like Lucy?" He drove without looking at her.

Cathy turned wide brown eyes on him, opened her mouth to speak, then closed it again.

Luke continued to drive, pretending not to notice her surprise, or not to heed. Then he commented casually. "You two have been at odds since you met."

"Well there's certainly no competition." Cathy muttered as she concentrated on her clenched hands in her lap.

"Lucy isn't my type."

The words triggered an emotional turmoil that caused Cathy to speak almost against her will. The words tumbled out breathlessly. "What is your type?"

He had stopped for a red light. Momentarily he turned sparkling green eyes and a warm smile in her direction. He spoke quietly. "I'll know when I find it." When the light changed to green he turned his full attention back to driving.

Not knowing why Cathy persisted. "Oh, come off it, Luke. You can't tell me you haven't noticed your assistant's figure. Why, she could have been a model." Cathy wriggled in her seat belt, reached up to remove her glasses and wipe perspiration from the bridge of her nose. She laid her spectacles on her dress and dropped her hands.

He commented. "Superficial." Then he gave her a sideways glance before continuing. "You're only looking at the surface, the physical beauty. There is a whole other concept that you are not seeing. There is natural beauty that is...instinctive, if you want to call it that. Then there is the spiritual beauty which come from within yourself, like the fruits of the Spirit, such as gentleness, kindness, peace…"

"Spirit?" Cathy interrupted. "Don't hand me that religious junk."

"I know, you don't understand. You will."

"Lucas, you are scaring me. I hate that feeling. Just like the other day when…" She bit her bottom lip to stop her tongue.

Luke eased the car into a parking space, turned off the engine, then turned to face her after unbuckling his seat belt. She was shaking her head, trying to avoid him, but his hands grasped her shoulders and turned her to face him. He gazed into her frightened features. "Cathy, tell me what happened to you."

Unable to stop the tears Cathy reached up to cover her eyes with both hands. "You'll think I'm crazy." She blurted out. Then she began to shake with sobs.

With a gentle, feather–like touch, he began to wipe the tears from her cheeks with soothing fingers. He murmured softly to her until she had calmed somewhat. "Let me help you, Cathy."

Finally she was able to speak. "It was so weird. I was walking through the alley on my way home after I left your office the other afternoon, when I saw someone behind me. This person was wearing long sleeves and pants, dressed all in black, like exercise clothing. I couldn't tell if it was a man or a woman. Anyway, the person ducked into a doorway when I spotted…it. Then, a few minutes later, when I turned the corner, I saw someone dressed just like that only wearing a cat mask and black hood. It blocked my way for a second. I looked around. Then, when I looked back, it was gone. Just like that. I…I…almost didn't believe it myself."

"Cathy, why didn't you stay on the street and go through the park?"

"Short cut."

"You won't be walking alone again. I'll see to that."

She sighed and looked at him. "Luke, you're not my big brother, you know. You can't be with me all the time."

"Hmm."

"What?" Cathy wore a bewildered look.

"Nothing. Come on, we'd better go eat. I'm certainly doing a lousy job of lifting your spirits." He reached over to unbuckle her seat belt then turned to step out of the car.

As they settled into a table for two Luke observed, "This is better. Thank God for air conditioning."

Cathy nodded briefly as a smiling waitress approached to take their orders. She hardly noticed the piano playing near by their table. After the woman had gone Cathy spoke honestly to her companion. "Luke, you know I'm not looking forward to that Bible meeting. I hope it wasn't a mistake agreeing to it. If Jess hadn't insisted, well, I don't know." She shrugged her shoulders.

Luke nodded then answered. "Yes, and I am very appreciative of you doing this. Some of the people who attend meetings are also my patients, I mean, their animals are. I think you will feel more relaxed once you meet them."

She still looked doubtful.

"Trust me, Cat." Then his tone of voice altered. "I wouldn't try ta buffalo ya, ma'am."

The poor yankee attempt to imitate western twang made her laugh.

Luke approved. "Now that's much better. A joyful heart is good medicine."

Cathy sighed and smiled at him. She picked up her soft

drink then asked, "Is that your prescription, Dr. Hoffman?"

"Actually, it's a Proverb."

She set her drink back down after sipping it then gazed into his eyes. "Got any more?"

He nodded and spoke softly. His gaze was still intent upon her. "The light of the eyes rejoices the heart:" Luke paraphrased the King James version of Proverbs 15:30.

She whispered, "Then your heart must be very glad." Those green orbs beckoned her to lose herself in their glow. Cathy found herself wishing she could capture some of his joy, but like had always been so uncertain for her. As if sensing her need, his hand came across the table to pat hers briefly. When he drew his away, caution growled in the pit of her stomach.

He was speaking. "Come, eat, you've barely touched your lunch."

Cathy managed to tear her gaze away from his eyes and look down. She picked up her sandwich to nibble at it. When she peered at him again, he was smiling.

He commented. "You eat slower than a cow."

She made a noise of protest and laughter, then took a larger bite.

Luke glanced at his watch. "We'll try to arrive early tonight, although I can't promise that."

"We?" She barely opened her lips to speak as she chewed.

"Mm. I'm picking Lucy up first. She really surprised me offering to come to the meeting. I've asked her plenty of times but she's never wanted to go before. I wonder why now?"

Cathy made a noise but said nothing. Surely he isn't that naive she told herself. Then she thought of her friend. After swallowing another bite she spoke. "Thank you for being nice to

Jess. She really is a dear once you get to know her."

"So are you."

She pulled her glass forward to stare at it's contents avoiding his gaze. "That's d–e–a–r." She spelled. When he didn't answer she glanced up. He was smiling and nodding. Luke waited patiently for her to finish eating before rising to leave the restaurant with her. He had driven her home before going back to his office and, before he left, he told her how much he had enjoyed her company. He made her promise to join him in the future. He made her feel happy and important. But, a little voice inside her warned her about her elated feelings.

Cathy had invited Jess to have supper with her that evening. She hoped the company would help relieve her nervousness about the up coming gathering. They were washing dishes when the door bell rang. Cathy sighed, put down her dish towel and went to answer it. She had mixed feelings when she opened the door to see Lucas standing with Lucy wrapped around his arm. She stepped aside and gestured for them to enter. Luke's smile was dazzling as always. She told them, "Jess and I were just finishing up dishes in the kitchen."

"Go ahead." Lucy encouraged as she lounged on the sofa. "Luke, where are you going?"

"Be right back." He responded over his shoulder as he followed Cathy into the kitchen. He greeted Cathy's friend with a smile. "Hi, Jess. It's good to see you again. Mm, coffee smells delicious, Cathy."

She nodded silently.

Then he asked her quietly, "Any more strange happenings, Cathy?"

"No, not lately."

Again the door bell sounded. This time Cathy greeted the building manager Max Frazer.

"I got the night off so I could come." He explained briefly.

"Oh? I didn't know you had another job as well?"

"There's a lot you don't know, Miss Lein."

She tried to ignore his pointed remark. "Well, since we are neighbors and all, you should call me Cathy. Come in and sit down."

Several guests later, the leader of the group study, John Helper arrived with his wife Elsie, who brought several tins of cookies which she had made herself. Luke offered to take them into the kitchen in order to speak with Cathy privately.

"Cathy, you'll see, these two really do live up to their name." Luke told her. "Any time you need a friend you can count on the three of us. John and Elsie have children of their own, but they are my very close friends and I hope they will be yours also, in time."

When they returned to the living room Cathy expressed her polite greetings.

"Luke has told us about you, Cathy." The older woman had a slightly high pitch to her pleasant voice. We want to especially thank you for having us here this evening. We hope you will want to join and become a part of our little group."

Cathy replied. "Well, I don't know."

Elsie's husband chided her. "Now, Elsie, give her a chance. Let the lady make up her own mind. She don't even know us yit. As fer what Lucas says, why, we'd be obliged to help anybody who needed it."

Somehow the accent didn't seem to fit a Bible scholar Cathy thought to herself. She glanced at Luke with a slight crease wrinkling her brow. Then she replied to the speaker. "Thank you, Mr. Helper, that is very kind of you. I will remember."

The stouter black man was already shaking his head. "Now, none of that mister stuff. It's just ol' John and Elsie, ya hear?"

Cathy smiled and nodded.

"Here, I'll write our names and phone number down for you, dear." Elsie offered and rose to comply. She wrote in small, neat lettering on the pad by Cathy's phone which she had placed on an end table in the living room. The answering machine was still hooked to her bed room extension and would faithfully record all calls. Cathy could check and delete unwanted ones after the guests had gone.

Again the door bell announced another arrival. Cathy excused herself to answer it. She was pleased to meet someone new from her own apartment building. By the time everyone had settled down and John stood to open the meeting, almost two dozen adults were present.

John began. "First off, we want to thank the Lord Jesus Christ for bringin' us all together to have fellowship with Him. Where two or three are gathered in His name, He is right smack in the middle of 'em. Second, we folks want to thank Miss Cathy Lein for invitin' us here this evening. For those of yeh who don't know me, I am John Helper and I like to keep it plain and simple, so it ain't hard to git the point. Elsie and I have a daughter who is naturally slow, so we like to keep things simple. Luke, would you start the readin' in Dan'el chapter five, so the folks who don't have the Good Book kin know what we're talkin' about?"

"I can't read." Jess said out loud as Luke stood with his Bible open to begin at verse five through verse 28.

"That's all right, Jess." Elsie, who was sitting next to the red head, patted her hand.

Luke then cleared his throat and began to speak. "This chapter is commonly referred to as The Writing on the Wall. Then he started to read the passages. When he had finished he briefly explained some background to the reading. Then he sat down.

Next John asked, "Now, would anyone like to take a guess as to what the lesson is here?"

"God's way or die." Cathy was surprised at her own bluntness. She quickly covered her mouth with her hand. She wished she hadn't spoken.

After a little pause of silence John stated. "That sounds a might bitter. Anyone else care to rephrase it?"

Elsie stood. "I'll try. If we ignore God's laws and try to go our own way, it eventually leads to death." She spoke slowly and clearly. "But, if we obey God, it leads to happiness and eternal reward." She sat down.

Then a male voice asked, "How do we know there is eternal reward?"

"An excellent question, Max." Luke stood and turned to John. "I'll take this one, okay?" The leader, his friend, nodded and Luke continued. "Sometimes, it may seem like the animals have one up on us, because they obey by instinct. It is natural for them. Our human nature, on the other hand, is born sinful, ready to disobey God. That's why He gave us His Word, the Bible, which guides us into His truth and plan for mankind. 'For all have sinned and come short of the glory of God.' That's from the book of Romans 3:23. Only by accepting God's free gift of eternal life through His Son Jesus Christ, who became a living sacrifice for us, can we hope to regain a right relationship with God the

Father and live forever in a perfect world." Luke paused to catch his breath then continued. "Romans 6:23 explains it. 'For the wages of sin is death, but the free gift of God is eternal life in Christ Jesus our Lord.' As for our reward," he began to turn pages then handed his book to Lucy, instructing her to read where he pointed.

"...'knowing that from the Lord you will receive your reward of the inheritance.' Luke, that's not a complete thought." Lucy turned wide blue circles in his direction.

He nodded then turned around to look at his audience and explained. "The point is that although there are many verses that talk about our reward, if we remain faithful and obedient, even until death, God has promised we will receive our inheritance of His kingdom along with His Son Jesus, who is our Savior and Lord. But, this must be a personal choice and each individual who has ever been born is given the opportunity to make this very decision."

"Luke, I have a question."

He turned with a smile toward the speaker. "What is it, Cathy?"

"Why such an elaborate show? I mean, foreign handwriting that had to be interpreted and this Daniel was the only one who knew the interpretation?"

"I can answer that." A meekly soft voice responded.

John encouraged, "Go ahead, Ruth."

Cathy watched a trim figure with silver gray hair and creamy white complexion stand to answer softly. "God had to use drastic means to get the king's attention. And, like this king who was murdered that evening, we need to make that choice, as soon as possible when it is offered to us. No one except the

Lord himself knows when death might occur, to any of us." She nodded her head shortly then resumed her seat.

John observed. "Good point. Now, let's pray." He bowed his head and folded his hands where he stood and began a prayer in which he invited those who would believe to accept God's free gift of salvation from sin in the person of Jesus Christ the Lord and Savior. Silence followed. After several minutes, John concluded the session with a prayer of thanksgiving and suggested singing before they broke for refreshments.

Cathy let out a long breath of relief. The seriousness of the conversation was making her feel uncomfortable. Her heartbeat quickened as Luke came to sit next to her.

"Share a hymn book with me?" Luke offered.

Cathy saw Lucy sit up straighter on the sofa, but she dared not look at the blonde's face. Her own voice began to stammer when she spoke. "I...I...don't know, Luke. I have to...to...look...awfully close...to see."

"That's okay."

John announced, "I'd like to start with What a Friend We Have in Jesus." Then he cited the numbered reference for the song.

Cathy spoke softly to Luke. "Jess has a beautiful singing voice." She looked up to see him nod. She also saw a twinkle sparkle in those adoring green eyes. Her heart ached to understand the light she beheld when she looked at the handsome man who was now sitting beside her. At this moment, she wished that he would stay with her and never leave. His presence lifted her spirits so.

Following several contemporary Christian songs, Elsie Helper stood to speak. "I'd like to call everyone's attention to this lovely young woman sitting next to me. Jess has recently moved here. She is on her own for the first time. Although she is developmentally disabled, like our daughter, she has her own apartment. I have been listening to her singing and I think such a beautiful voice deserves to be shared. She says she knows Jesus Loves Me, so I asked her to stand and sing it for us. John will accompany Jess on his guitar." She sat and began to clap. The other people did also. She then touched Jess'es arm. "Stand up, dear." Elsie prompted.

After her song, the audience needed no prodding to show their appreciation for someone with natural talent. The rousing applause brought a gleeful giggle from the young woman.

When the group had quieted John stood. "Such a wonderful singing group needs to be rewarded. I hear tell of coffee and desserts. Now let me just sum up and we'll eat. I think Hebrews 11:6 makes the point of this lesson clear. I'll read it. 'And without faith it is impossible to please Him, for he who comes to God must believe that He is and that He is a rewarder of those who seek Him.' Thank you. That's it folks."

Cathy had to admit to herself that although she had felt uncomfortable at first, she had a much better time than she could have imagined. The treats alone were worth the pressure she had felt. Of course, Lucas being near...No no, her mind warned. Can't afford to start those feelings. How could this Jesus make such a difference in a persons life she wondered? What was this special glow that seemed to permeate these people? She nibbled happily at her goodies. Again that soothing masculine voice came, like a melody, to her ears.

"I'd love to know what you are thinking, Cat."

She blinked and wriggled a bit on her chair as she felt the

color rise in her cheeks. She made a small sound and then admitted, "Well, Lucas, I was thinking about you." Courageously she resolved to look upward. A smile spread across her lips. His bewildered expression told her that he was at a loss for words. Feeling a touch of cattiness she ventured, "Cat got your tongue, Luke?"

He laughed heartily and shook his head. Finally he remarked, "Careful now, that old line can have other interpretations."

It was Cathy's turn to shake her head. "I don't understand."

Turning his face away he pushed his hand through the wavy locks of hair to hide the coloring to his own features. "If we were alone I'd show you." He chided himself for the strength of his feeling, wanting to kiss her.

Cathy's smile faded as Lucy approached them. "Here comes your date, Luke."

His head came up as Lucy's hand touched his shoulder.

"There you are, Luke, honey. I've been looking all over for you."

To herself Cathy scolded, "What's the matter? Need to sharpen your claws?" Aloud she managed a cordial greeting.

Lucy's fingers tightened and she spoke to the man ignoring Cathy. "C'mon, Luke. It's getting late and people are leaving."

He and Cathy both looked around. If anyone had left, it had gone unnoticed by the majority of the gathering. Then he spoke. "Be patient, Lucy. Here, I'll get you some more coffee." He took Lucy's empty cup and then turned to the other woman. "Cathy?"

Seizing her opportunity, Cathy nodded and smiled warmly.

The blonde tossed her head in a hands off gesture and stood with hands on her hips.

For conversations sake Cathy asked, "Well, Lucy, what made you decide to become a veterinarian's assistant?"

"I am interested in breeding." The high feminine voice replied.

I'll bet you are, Cathy thought. Aloud she asked, "Do you have animals?"

The other female tossed her hair and answered "I have two springer spaniels and I hope to have a litter to sell some time this year."

Cathy responded, "I'd like to have a cat someday."

Lucy made a disgusting noise then muttered "Figures."

When Luke returned they both smiled and thanked him.

"I told her about Dora and Teddy, Luke." Lucy chattered. "So when Dora becomes pregnant, she'll have to be right by that phone, in case I need you."

"Hey..." Cathy began to speak, but Luke interrupted her.

"Lucy, don't worry. Everything will be fine. Cathy doesn't have to be put under such scrutiny. You had my home number before she did. Don't worry. Both of you will be able to reach me if ever you need to. I promise."

"Why does she—" Lucy stopped in mid sentence apparently thinking better of her protest. She then gulped down her coffee. "Ready to go now, Luke?"

"In a few minutes, Lucy. I want to speak to our hostess alone first." He took Cathy's elbow and guided her toward the kitchen.

"Looks like Jess and Elsie are becoming fast friends." Cathy commented as they walked past the two who were seated beside each other but separate from the larger group. She dared not speculate on this man's intentions. Yet, her heart was pounding as if she had just run a mile in record time. When they entered the kitchen she closed the door behind them and turned to face him.

"Cathy, I want to thank you sincerely for doing this for me tonight. I truly appreciate it." His eyes sought hers. "Also, I want you to call me at any time. I mean it. I don't like these strange things that have been happening to you."

She made a small sound of exclamation. "Luke, I had almost forgotten." She blinked as memory brought back the image of the cat like figure in the alley and the dead cat on her fire escape. Her expression must have mirrored her thoughts. Suddenly all thoughts shattered like glass breaking apart and floating freely as arms and lips claimed her intensely. She responded, drawn by the magnetism of his kiss.

When their lips parted, he murmured softly, "Thank you, dear." Then he drew back and turned to move toward the closed door.

Cathy took a step forward to stand where the man had stood. She touched her tongue to her lips and breathed in his lingering scent. What made this man so different than any other she had met? Even when Jim had kissed her she had not been bombarded by such a flood of emotions. It had been warm and pleasant, but that was all. Lucas seemed to evoke the best and the worst of her hopes and fears all at the same time. She had no idea how long she had stood there, but her pondering was interrupted by the door bell.

When she opened the door, Cathy had to fight the urge to jump into Luke's arms. She grasped one of his hands and spoke quickly. "Come in, Luke." In her excitement she finally realized that she was tugging, but he was not yielding to her invitation.

"What's wrong?"

Luke explained as he continued to hold onto her hand. "Cathy, there is something that you need to see. Come with me."

"I'll just get my door key. Are we going outside?"

He released her hand and shook his head. He waited there while she retrieved it and came to lock the apartment door behind her. Then he told her, "There is some...uh...descriptive writing on the wall in the laundry room. The light was on in there when Lucy and I passed it. I came back to get you. You'll see."

She followed him silently as she felt his dead seriousness.

When they arrived Lucy and Jess were standing inside the laundry room. Jess pointed to the wall beside the row of washers.

Jess said, "Look at that. Just like the writing on the wall in the Bible story. Do you think God did it?"

"Hardly." Lucy managed to turn a beginning laugh into a word.

Silently Cathy read:

Adult in body, but child in mind.

Reminiscent of innocence sublime.

Can't turn back the hands of time.

T'was truly frail, this feline.

"What does it mean?" Jess asked.

"We don't know." Lucy answered. Then she added, "None of us wrote it."

Jess asked, "Who's it for?"

Cathy looked at her friend and then re read the first line to herself. She turned fearful eyes toward her male companion.

"Oh, Luke, it can't be."

"Lord, I hope not." He petitioned. "Cathy, I'm going to take Jess to her apartment and Lucy home, then I'll come back. Call the police in the meantime."

Lucy protested. "Really, Luke, it's just a dumb prank."

"Go back and lock your door, Cathy." Luke advised.

Cathy nodded and turned to go. She knew that Jess did not grasp their thoughts and she was thankful for that. There was no comfort in the fact that Luke shared her concern that her special friend Jess might be in danger.

5. A Common Bond

Cathy felt she had waited long enough. Luke hadn't come back so she went ahead and cleaned the large coffee maker, put it away for another occasion, and taken her shower. It was almost midnight when she sat on the edge of her bed to brush her hair. Then the telephone screamed at her. Cathy put down her brush to answer it. There was no response.

"Lein's Line. May I help you?" She repeated.

A hissing sound met her ear.

"Who is this?" She almost yelled it into the mouth piece.

Ragged breathing followed. She was about to remove the phone from her ear when the sound changed to an authentic reproduction of cat's purring.

"What is going on?" She asked.

The answer was the familiar click, then she was left with nothing. She sat, holding the receiver above her lap, until the chime of the door bell intruded. Cathy stood, replaced the receiver in it's cradle, then headed for the living room, tying the belt to her robe tighter as she walked. At the door she paused. "Who is there?"

"Cathy, it's Luke Hoffman."

Hurriedly now she unlocked and opened the door.

"Oh, I am sorry. I didn't mean to get you out of bed. I didn't realize the time."

"No, you didn't. Luke, please stay awhile. I just got another one of those weird calls." She relocked the door, then went to replay the message on the answering machine for him. When they went back into the living room she sat beside him on the couch.

"Maybe the FBI should put a tap on your phone, Cathy." Luke suggested.

She speculated. "I don't know if they would. No crime has been committed."

He told her, "That's what the policeman said when I showed him the writing on the wall in the laundry room. He was in the hall when I came back. That's why it took me so long. I didn't know if I should have come."

She admitted, "I'm glad you did. It's getting scary."

His arms were encircling her with warmth and encouragement. With a sigh she settled against him and rested her head on his broad shoulder.

He spoke quietly. "Cathy, you and Jess shouldn't be out walking alone, even in daylight."

"Mm. Then you do think Jess might be in danger too." She moved her head to look up.

He nodded. "I don't want anything to happen to her or you."

"Thanks." She replied softly. A common bond of caring had strengthened their relationship. However, Cathy was still unnerved by how comfortable and natural she felt in this man's arms.

Several days later Cathy received a call from Elsie Helper

inviting her and Jess to come to their farm for a visit. Cathy had explained that a week day would be better as she was on call evenings and week ends. Elsie had allowed Cathy to set up the date. When the day arrived, Elsie picked them up in a pick up truck after her children had left for day camp.

As they walked toward the barn Jess asked, "Where is John?"

Elsie explained. "He works for a tractor company down the road. He is a mechanic. He fixes tractors and other equipment."

Cathy said, "Then he has a good job. He farms too?"

Elsie smiled and nodded. "He loves it. Don't let his manner of speech fool you. John is an educated man. He just likes to talk, as he puts it, 'natural like'. He says that writin' and talkin' are two different animals."

Jess asked, "How many kids did you say you have?"

"We have eight living with us now, but they are not all our own. John and I are foster parents. We take in other displaced children. Our biological children are Jack, the oldest, and Ella, who is like you, Jess. I want you to meet her especially. You both are very sweet."

"Thank you, Elsie. It must take a lot of patience." Jess commented. "Oh, look! Can I pet the cow? I have never seen a real cow up close."

Elsie nodded.

Next, Jess asked, "Does Dr. Hoffman take care of your animals when they are sick?"

Again Elsie nodded. "He also cares for them when they are well. They need shots to stay healthy just like human children do. He also cares for them when they have babies."

Cathy grabbed her opportunity. "How long have you known

Luke?"

"Oh, about three years now, I guess. We've been with him since he started his practice here in Manchester when he was fresh out of medical school."

They walked through the large barn and continued outside at the father end. Elsie continued, "God had His hand in it if you ask me. Our long time vet, Dr. Bishop, was getting ready to retire, so he applied to the University of New Hampshire for a replacement he could train. Luke was one of the candidates among the graduate students who applied. The doctor took a liking to him right away. You see, Luke has a heart for his work, a rare and precious trait."

Cathy nodded her agreement. "Yes, I know."

Elsie asked, "You like him then?"

The question was innocent enough, but Cathy was wary of revealing her feelings, even to herself. But she was finding him more and more attractive as time passed. Finally she said, hoping to sound casual, "He is a very nice man."

Elsie agreed.

Then Cathy asked, "Have you met his assistant Lucy Becker?"

"Briefly. I don't know about you two ladies, but I am getting tired of walking. Come into the house for some refreshments."

As Elsie turned to lead the way, Cathy took another look out over the grassy fields dotted with cows enjoying the sunshine. Cathy persisted as they walked back through the barn. "So you don't know Lucy very well?"

"No, why. Have you made friends with her already?" Elsie asked.

Cathy covered her mouth to stifle a laugh with a cough.

When she regained her composure she answered honestly. "Hardly that. We are more like rivals—that is, in her mind anyway." Cathy quickly amended her sentence.

"Luke doesn't say much about her at all." Elsie held the screen door for them to enter the large kitchen. Then she told them. "He has spoken of you though, Cathy, often."

Grateful for a diversion, Cathy fixed her eyes on a large multicolored lump of fur perched on the windowsill. "Oh, what a beautiful cat. May I touch it?"

"Oh sure." Elsie replied delightedly. "Missy loves to be fussed over, like most women."

Jess asked, "Can I hold her?"

Cathy grasped the large animal under her feet and lifted her slowly into her arms. She extended one hand to gently stroke the soft fur and tickle under the v shaped chin with one finger. She was rewarded with loud rumbling from the cat's throat. Cathy walked slowly to the table where Jess sat and placed the bundle in her lap. "Be gentle, Jess. Don't move too fast."

Her companion giggled happily as the animal contentedly settled into a more comfortable position. Missy continued to purr happily as Jess petted and fondled her.

Elsie brought iced tea and home made muffins to the table before sitting down herself. She smiled appreciatively and then spoke. "Animals know when they are loved."

Cathy sighed then asserted, "It's more complicated with people, isn't it?"

Elsie observed wisely, "Sometimes they make it so."

Without thinking about it Cathy admitted, "I was raised in an orphanage."

Elsie also spoke candidly. "Yes, dear, Luke told us."

Jess broke the somber moment by stating how much she enjoyed the treats as she chewed.

"Thank you, Jess."

Cathy watched Elsie pause and bow her head quietly, as Luke had done, before she ate or drank anything. Again Cathy ventured to be bold. "It sounds like you think very highly of Luke." She then dropped her gaze to examine the contents of her tall glass.

"Yes, both John and I know the kind of man he is."

This statement brought Cathy's eyes back to the darker woman's face. "Now you've got me curious, Elsie. That's quite a statement."

Elsie replied slowly. "It takes time to get to know someone well. But, believe me, you won't be sorry if you do. He's worth the time."

Jess asked, "How long did you and John go out?"

Cathy smiled at her friend's uncanny perception.

"Before we got married?" Elsie asked.

Jess nodded.

"Let me see, it was almost a year before we became engaged. Then we were married a couple of months after that."

Then Jess asked, "How did you know you loved John?"

Cathy coughed as she swallowed her tea. When she recovered she spoke first. "Jess, if she could answer that one, she could be a rich woman. Everyone wants the answer to that question."

Elsie chuckled quietly then she answered in turn. "God knows the heart, Jess. If you are trusting Him, He will let you know when it is right."

Cathy shook her head and refused to speak. She was

relieved when Elsie changed the subject to more neutral ground. "I wrote up some quick recipes if you two would like to have them."

"But I..."

Cathy interrupted her friend. "Yes, that's nice of you, Elsie. Jess and I can try them out together."

Jess agreed. "Gee, that sounds like fun."

When they were ready to leave, Elsie drove them back to their apartment building in the city of Manchester. Bedford was a suburban town just outside the city which still housed several farms. Cathy had thanked her and promised that she and Jess would visit again. She was grateful that neither Luke nor Elsie had pressed the religious issue. She wanted no part of that in her life. She found herself liking Elsie though. She was the most open woman Cathy had ever met, besides her friend Jess. No wonder Luke was so friendly with the Helpers. She shook her head. Her thoughts had again strayed to the handsome veterinarian. As she and Jess walked past the manager's office, she saw Max Frazer through the open door, apparently reading. She called casually to him.

"Hi, Max. What are you reading?"

His head jerked up as surprise snapped in his voice. "Poetry." The head lowered again.

Jess commented. "Grouchy ain't he?"

Cathy waved a dismissing hand as they walked. Nothing was going to ruin her happy mood.

Nothing except Dr. Paul Davis. He was on the other end of the line when she got back. Cathy had to slam the door and hurry to pick up the phone before the answering machine cut in. It was already ringing when she got home.

His voice snapped at her. "It's about time. Now, are you going to be dependable while I'm out to lunch? Or do I have to make my receptionist wait until I return?"

"I'll be right here, Dr. Davis. Is something wrong?"

"I performed in office surgery on a patient this morning. He is a hemophiliac, a bleeder."

Cathy started to explain that she knew what the word meant, but the doctor interrupted her.

"If Mr. Cooper has any problems someone will call." He named the restaurant where he would be and the time he expected to be away from the office. Then he hung up abruptly.

After checking to be sure she had locked the door, Cathy sighed and went to the kitchen to file her new recipes. When the phone rang again, she quickly answered it on the kitchen extension.

"Cathy, it's Luke. I was wondering if you are free for lunch?"

Her heartbeat had quickened. "No, I'm so sorry, I can't today. One of my clients has an emergency case and I must be on call for him while he is away."

"No problem. I understand. Are you free this evening? I mean, can I bring supper and a movie? We could watch it while we eat, say...Chinese?"

"Really? Oh, that would be wonderful, Luke. You know, Jess and I visited with Elsie Helper this morning. She is such an open person. I've never known anyone like that, I mean, except you."

"Ah, yes, I told you she and John live up to their name. I'll see you this evening around six?"

Cathy agreed and they said good–bye for the time being. She hadn't told him about the recipes. Cathy resolved to try her hand at baking for a surprise. The afternoon passed quickly and quietly.

When Luke arrived, he brought an assortment of delicacies and Chinese tea. The DVD, he said, was a romance, but he neglected to tell her that it had a Christian theme. They were enjoying their meal when the phone interrupted them. Cathy went to answer.

"Luke, it's your kennel staff worker."

He rose to take the phone. After a short time of listening he responded quietly. "I'm on my way. Cathy I have to go. An older dog that we are caring for is having trouble. You watch the rest of the movie. I'm sorry, Cat."

She nodded her understanding as he left.

Once the movie had finished, Cathy was glad to be alone. She wanted to be angry at him for bringing a movie that was Christian in nature, but it had been so moving. It had evoked an emotional response from her. When she had put away the remainder of the food and went to the microwave oven to reheat her tea, Cathy realized that Luke didn't get the opportunity to sample her baking project. Then the front door bell sounded. When she asked who it was, Luke responded.

Upon opening the door, she found his expression to be sullen. Immediately she showed concern. He began by apologizing.

"I didn't know if I should come back this late. I just didn't want to go home right away. I felt like talkin' to someone."

She tried to reassure him. "I'm glad you came, Luke."

He paced back and forth in front of the couch. "There was nothing I could do. The dog was 13 years old. His heart just gave out."

Perhaps a month ago Cathy would have been insensitive to

the death of an animal unknown to her. But she cared about the feelings of this kind and sensitive man, even more than she was willing to admit to herself. She had never met a man like him before. Now she came and put her arms around him. "I am so sorry, Luke."

Luke responded to her embrace and rested his forehead on her shoulder. After a deep sigh, he told her that he would have to call the male's owners in the morning. They were aware of the circumstances but their dog had been a loyal and loving companion to the elderly couple, not just a pet. Then he added, "I know I shouldn't let it get to me, but I..." His voice cracked, so he fell silent.

Cathy tightened her embrace. She did not know what to do for solace. She hoped she was a comfort to him. Then she tried to think of something to take his mind off the grief he was experiencing. After a time he sighed and lifted his head. It was then she asked, "Luke, do animals go to Heaven?" She could see that he was surprised by the question.

Encouraged, he answered. "No one really knows but I certainly hope so. We know that only men and women have the ability to choose their destinies. Animals and plants, other living things, have been given natural instincts by God but they don't have to make a choice. The Bible does indicate in Romans 8:19–23 that creation waits for God to perfect His plan." As he talked, Luke removed his small Bible from his shirt pocket. "It says: 'For the anxious longing of the creation waits eagerly for the revealing of the sons of God. For the creation was subjected to futility, not willingly, but because of Him who subjected it, in hope that the creation itself also will be set free from its slavery to corruption into the freedom of the glory of the children of

God. For we know that the whole creation groans and suffers the pains of childbirth together until now. And not only this, but also we ourselves, having the first fruits of the Spirit, even we ourselves groan within ourselves, waiting eagerly for our adoption as sons, the redemption of our body.' There are several passages in Isaiah which refer to animals."

They went to sit together on the couch as Luke continued to explain. He turned to the book of Isaiah to read:

"Isaiah 11: 6–9, 'And the wolf will dwell with the lamb, And the leopard will lie down with the young goat, And the calf and the young lion and the fatling together; And a little boy will lead them. Also the cow and the bear will graze, Their young will lie down together, And the lion will eat straw like the ox. The nursing child will play by the hole of the cobra, And the weaned child will put his hand on the viper's den. They will not hurt or destroy in all My holy mountain, For the earth will be full of the knowledge of the Lord. As the waters cover the sea.' Isaiah 65:25, 'The wolf and the lamb will graze together, and the lion will eat straw like the ox; and dust will be the serpent's food They will do no evil or harm in all My holy mountain," says the Lord.'" Luke looked up from the book as he turned pages. Now, there is just one more place I want to read. Here it is. It's from the book of Luke 12: 6–7 'Are not five sparrows sold for two cents? Yet not one of them is forgotten before God. Indeed, the very hairs of your head are all numbered. Do not fear; you are more valuable than many sparrows.' That's it for now, Cat."

"Wow." Cathy exclaimed. "I never gave anything like that a thought before."

Luke closed his pocket Bible and replaced it in his shirt pocket. Then he ventured, "So, you believe in Heaven, Cat?"

"Well, I really don't know. I do believe in a Creator. I mean, we had to begin somewhere. I've always heard about Jesus being God's Son and the creation story and some of the other Bible events but I never heard Him referred to as a person, I mean, personally, the way you and Elsie and John do. Oh, by the way, Luke, you never got to sample my creation." She smiled at his inquisitive look. She stood and reached for his hand. "I got some recipes from Elsie this morning. I made us some cookies and pastries. There is still some tea left. Come into the kitchen with me. We can have dessert after all."

He also stood and took her outstretched hand. As they proceeded, the corners of his mouth now curved upward in a faint smile.

6. Invitations

The summer turned into autumn all too quickly. Cathy's business grew as time passed. Days became cooler and shorter with the seasonal change. She and Jess had gone several more times to visit Elsie Helper. Jess and her daughter Ella were becoming friends. Ella began a new job at a workshop for the handicapped in Manchester and Jess also decided to try her hand at this new venture. This gave Cathy more free time for herself during week days since Jess began work full time. Her income would be minimal but the experience would be valuable.

One crisp morning Cathy had left the apartment early to run errands. When she returned near the lunch hour, she smelled coffee perking as she entered the building. Seeing the open door of the manager's office, she commented as she passed. "Mm smells delicious, Max."

The man looked up from his paper work. "How about joinin' me in a cup, Cathy?"

She hesitated a moment, then accepted his offer. She felt chilly from the autumn air. She smiled as she entered the office to sit down. "Thank you. It is turning colder outside.

He nodded. "Been shopping?"

She shook her head. "No, I just had some errands to run. I thought I'd get it over with early and get back inside where it's warm."

He rose to fill their cups when the coffee had finished perking. "I didn't know I was going to have company. But, I am glad you stopped in."

"Thank you." She replied casually.

He returned to the table with their cups. They carried on a light conversation mostly about the weather while they drank. When she had finished, Cathy thanked him and rose to leave saying, "I should get back in case anyone calls during lunchtime."

He nodded and said good–bye.

Cathy was actually beginning to miss her visits with Elsie Helper since the older lady was back teaching school again now. She found that she had plenty of time to catch up on her bookkeeping and housekeeping with all of her newly acquired friends, Luke, Elsie and now Jess, having daily activities to occupy them. Even her Wednesday evenings were quiet since Luke attended church weekly on these evenings. Oh, stop feeling sorry for yourself, she mentally chided. Might think you couldn't make more friends or fend for yourself as you used to do. Still, she felt a growing emptiness within that Cathy didn't understand.

She was watching television on one of those empty Wednesday evenings when the phone rang a little after 9:30.

"Lein's Answering Line. May I help you?" She answered cheerfully. It was Luke.

"Cathy, I was wondering if you would let us have another Bible study at your place?"

"Oh, uh, yes. That will be alright."

"Really? That's great. I was wondering, would tomorrow night be too soon?"

"Well, I guess not."

"Oh, thank you, Cat. That's great. I'll call around and set it up, okay?"

"Yes. I'll see you tomorrow night then."

He thanked her again and was about to hang up the phone when she spoke.

"Luke, I was wondering..." She let her sentence lapse.

"Yes, I'm listening, Cathy."

"Remember, in the restaurant, what you said about the heart being joyful? Can we read something like that tomorrow?"

Luke's voice was full with delight. "Oh, you liked the Proverbs. Of course, I remember. Sure we can. I'll let John know."

"Okay, bye for now." Her voice was quietly shy.

"Good night, Cat." He hung up the phone.

She sighed. Cathy had mixed feelings, but it would be good to see Elsie and John again as well. She went to the kitchen to check her supplies.

The next evening she greeted everyone cheerfully. To her delight, Luke arrived alone. Lucy did not join him this time. Elsie and John also brought their daughter Ella who sat with Jess. Once everyone was seated John opened the meeting by thanking Cathy for having the group again.

"Now, I hear we have a special request to study in the book of Proverbs tonight, so let's turn to chapter..." John looked over at Luke who supplied the number, then he continued, "...seventeen. Cathy, would you like to begin reading fer us? Go 'till the end of this chapter." John sat.

Luke handed Cathy his Bible opened to the proper place. Obediently she stood and began to read aloud. Her voice was mid range in pitch and clearly easy to hear. A slight eagerness was apparent to the listeners as she read the passages for the first time. When she had finished she commented, "I like these sayings." Then she sat down again.

John stood. "Thank you, Cathy. That was delightful listenin' to ya. But, these are more than sayin's. They are God's truths to live by. That is why He gave us His Word. It is a guide for us to folla. 'Your Word is a lamp to my feet and a light for my path.' That's a quote from Psalms 119:105." John explained. "Now, does anyone else have anything to say before we continue our readin' in this lesson?"

Silence prevailed so John asked Ryan, one of the church deacons, to read the next chapter.

During refreshments Elsie confessed to Cathy that she wished there was a way Cathy could get some free time to attend their church. She had remarked that since Cathy seemed to enjoy the study group, she would surely feel the same about the church service. Cathy had merely shrugged her shoulders and nodded politely.

Cathy had to admit to herself that she did sincerely enjoy the company and the small group gathering. Everyone was so nice to each other. She had not been in such a pleasing atmosphere for any length of time in her past. Sometimes she was happy about it, but other times, she was fearful. Her stomach would knot and she was reminded to be careful with her feelings. Then there was Luke, that kind and gentle man who made her feel so inexplicably wonderful. What was to become of that? She dared not think along this line, but she couldn't stop her thoughts from straying to the man in her life.

One morning, soon after the second group gathering at her apartment, Cathy received a phone call from a woman.

"Hi, Cathy, I'm Tina Booth, one of tthe tenants in your building who came to the group study at your apartment. I was wondering if we might get together sometime to chat?"

"Yes, that sounds great, but can you come here?"

"Sure. I work, Saturdays so I get Mondays off. How about this coming Monday?"

"Yes, I'm free. How about around ten o'clock?"

"Fine. I'll be there."

Cathy was on her way toward the door of the apartment building to run errands when Max Frazer called from the office. "Hey, Cathy, where are you off to in such a hurry?"

She looked and turned back to answer that she had some errands.

"Want a ride?" He offered.

Her stomach began to tighten. She really didn't know this man very well. She thought for a moment then asked, "Don't you have to stay around the building?"

He shrugged his shoulders and replied. "A short time won't matter much."

"No, I don't think so." She shook her head, thanked him and turned to head outside.

The day was a crisp, cold Friday. The sun was shining, but it provided little warmth in New England autumn. The early mornings were frosty, hinting of the autumn color soon to paint the tree tops. Autumn was such a beautifully colorful time of year, in spite of the cold that warned of winter's approach. Cathy concentrated on thinking about her grocery list. She would be seeing Luke this evening and she also wanted to try her hand at baking again for her new acquaintance who would be visiting at the beginning of the week. She had forgotten Luke's warning not to venture out by herself. She felt confident as she waited for the bus to go down town.

Her day had been successful, without incident. She was putting her groceries away when the door bell rang. Cathy went to the front door and asked who was there.

"Delivery for Miss Cathy Lein."

"I didn't order anything." She responded.

"Lady, I got a delivery for you. I'm from the florist shop."

She sighed and unlocked the door. To her surprise she found a man standing there with a large bouquet of yellow roses. She took them, thanked him and relocked her door. She took them into the kitchen to add water to the vase and look for a card. Finding one she carefully removed and opened it. It read "Flowers for a lovely lady, Your Friend, Luke." She smiled with delight as she placed the vase in the center of the table.

Once she had finished in the kitchen Cathy went into the bedroom to change and freshen up before Luke's arrival. Cathy had previously pulled down the shade and closed the curtains. Following her luxuriously warm, soothing bath, as she was toweling her hair, Cathy happened to peek behind the shade to glance out of her bedroom window. It had been the beginning of twilight when she went into the bathroom. She suspected it was fully dark by now. She gasped at the sight which was clearly visible under luminance from the street light standing near the corner. She began to shiver but told herself to concentrate on what she was doing. Then she went to her closet to choose an outfit. She settled on a comfortable pant suit of cotton and polyester material. It was a beige color with yellow trim about the neck and sleeves. She slipped her feet into her yellow slippers. It was her favorite color.

When she greeted Luke at the door he was completely surprised to find her in tears.

"Cathy, I thought I would surprise you with the flowers, but I've never gotten quite this reaction before."

He had to wait for her to calm enough to explain. Finally she gestured toward her bedroom.

"Oh Luke, it happened again. Go look. It's on the fire escape."

He followed her to the room where she opened the curtains and drew up the shade. She stepped back. As Luke came forward, he saw, lying limp on the fire escape, another dead, pregnant cat. He picked up her phone to call the animal officer.

7. A Gift

When Monday morning arrived Cathy greeted Tina with eagerness at the door. She invited the young woman into the kitchen for coffee and pastries. Once they were seated at the table Tina commented.

"I was surprised to meet someone near my age. I am pleased to meet you Cathy."

"Yes, me too." Cathy agreed. She explained her answering service business and how she was usually tied up evenings and weekends, so getting together on a Monday worked out well for her.

"I'm a beautician at the shop in the mall. Although my hours change sometimes I always work every other week end and get Mondays off when I work Saturdays. Too bad you can't arrange something with another answering service so you can have every other weekend off." Tina suggested to Cathy.

"Yes, that is a good idea. I wonder if I can look into that. I'd like to have some free time on weekends now that I'm," she paused momentarily, wondering if she should reveal to this new acquaintance her budding relationship, but finally decided to go ahead, "I'm dating Dr. Luke Hoffman, the veterinarian." After all, Cathy thought to herself, Tina had come to the Bible study group. Maybe she already knew him and some of the others.

Tina nodded her head. "Yes, I know who you mean. What did you think of the group? I am a new Christian and I don't know much about the Bible yet. I really enjoyed the meetings. Didn't you? Well, you must have since you hosted them. Do you think I could do that as well?"

"Oh I'm sure you could. I don't know anything about the Bible myself either." Cathy admitted.

They chatted congenially as time passed quickly. Tina left around lunch time saying she had some errands to run and thanking Cathy for the refreshments. They vowed to get together again.

Cathy searched in the phone book for answering service businesses. She found another listing besides her own and ventured to call it. She spoke with a middle aged married woman who was delighted to find someone else in business who was willing to share alternate weekends. The woman used the business to help the family income and welcomed the opportunity to have backup support as Cathy did. Cathy also explained her situation. Cathy expressed her delight to the other woman, Penny Jones, and they exchanged necessary information before ending the call.

It was late afternoon, following house cleaning, when Cathy decided to call Elsie Helper and tell her the news. She felt a happy satisfaction as the day was progressing nicely. A short time later, to her delight, Luke called to make evening plans. Her spirits were soaring when she greeted him at the door.

"Cathy, may I say, you are looking very attractive." Luke noticed. She had loosely curled her hair and put on an attractive dress. She stepped closer to him. He drew her into close embrace and gave her an affectionate kiss. Then she pulled away.

She suggested, "Let's eat, shall we? Coffee's ready." She started toward the kitchen. She chatted happily while they ate, up dating him on her news.

Then Luke commented. "Well now, I guess that means I will be able to take you out sometimes on a real date."

She pounced. "Huh! Really? What would you call this? Haven't we been dating all along?"

"Sure we have. I just meant I can now take you out, say, to the theater, a concert, I don't know, bowling maybe. You know, things we can't do in an apartment. Oh Cathy, I'd love to take you to a county fair. I love the fairs. There's lots to see."

"That sounds nice. It's been ages since I've been to a play."

"And you won't have to worry about anything. I won't let anything happen to you, Cathy, I promise." His expression was serious. "You can trust me...completely."

"Okay." She said it slowly.

He continued. "I mean it. I wouldn't ask you to do anything against God's principles. I really enjoy being with you, Cathy."

"I feel the same way about you, Luke. You make me feel so...special. I can't explain it. But, trust is a big step. I almost trusted someone once...but it didn't work out well at all."

"Do you want to talk about it?" Luke asked.

She shrugged her shoulders. Then she told him about dating Jim Ashton who was a coworker at the group home in Hanover. When she had invited him to her apartment, he had tried to take advantage of her, and she had broken it off.

"You won't have to worry about that with me, Cathy. In fact, that is a big part of the foundation of a right relationship with God, trust. One of my favorite verses from Proverbs is about trust."

"A proverb?" She queried.

He nodded. "Proverbs 3:5–6, 'Trust in the Lord with all your heart and do not lean on your own understanding. In all your ways acknowledge Him, and He will make your paths straight.'"

Cathy stood to take their dishes to the kitchen. Then she looked over at him to answer. "That is asking a lot."

Luke also stood to help clear the table. He continued. "That's because you haven't experienced God's awesome love for us yet. He loved us so much that He sent His only begotten Son, Jesus, to take our sins upon Himself and become our living sacrifice so that we can gain back a right relationship with God our Father. Believe me, Cathy, if you desire to take that first step in trusting God and accept His free gift of life in His Son Jesus, you will be free from fear, sin, death and have life everlasting. As John Helper puts it, 'after that is the growin' process. That takes a life time.'"

"I don't know, Luke." Then she sighed.

He grinned a little then spoke. "As John would say, 'think on it awhile.' Okay?"

She smiled back at him. "Okay."

His kiss was warm, inviting, making her feel weak and pliable again. Afterward, she confessed to him while gazing into his eyes, "Luke, you make me feel all kinds of ways I've never felt before."

"Likewise." He murmured. Then he added, "Maybe God is trying to tell us something."

Several days later, about mid afternoon, there came a knock at her door. When she asked who it was a male voice told her she had a package delivery. She opened the door to see a man in uniform for the trucking company holding a long rectangle box.

She thanked him then closed and locked the door again. There was no return address on the label she noticed as she set it down on the coffee table in the living room. She retrieved a knife from the kitchen to open the box. Inside she found yellow flowers, wilted and dead. There was no card either. A few minutes later the phone rang. When she picked up the receiver she didn't have time to finish her greeting before slow grated words came back to her ear and the recorder:

Not that I loved too well or loved too much.
Would that again I could feel her touch.
Within my restless soul grows weary.
Why does love consume in fury?

Panic seized her and threatened to stricken her throat. Cathy went to the kitchen for a drink of cold water which she could feel all the way down her throat. She dialed the police station. Then she called Luke. Thankfully he arrived before the policeman. Luke had thoughtfully brought sub sandwiches and cold drinks, but Cathy was too upset to eat just then.

She asked meekly, "Why is someone doing this to me?"

Luke shook his head wordlessly. Anger and helplessness were churning inside him.

"The flowers were yellow, my favorite color. How could someone know that?"

"Coincidence?" Luke asked.

Cathy shook her head and shrugged her shoulders.

Luke said, "I'll put this food in your refrigerator for now, Cathy. Maybe you'll feel like eating after..." His sentence was interrupted by a knocking at her door. Luke went to the kitchen while she answered it. It was the police officer.

When Luke returned from the kitchen she introduced him. The officer listened to her story and took pictures of the box and its contents. Then he explained that there was no way to obtain finger prints from such items, but he would check with the package delivery companies in town to try to get an identification on a suspect. Then he asked if there was anything else she could add.

"Just that the flowers were my favorite color." Cathy supplied. Then she remembered. "Oh, wait a minute. The message on the answering machine. It was done in the same way as one I got before. She went to replay the tape.

Luke gasped when he heard the rhyme.

The officer asked for the tape as Cathy expected. She explained that the policeman had taken the previous similar message tape as well. The officer thanked her and said she would be contacted if anything resulted from the investigation but he was doubtful. There was not much to go on.

Cathy nodded and thanked him as he left. Once she had locked the door again Luke came to put his arms around her. She quivered in his embrace.

Luke held and cuddled her while his mind questioned and prayed. Finally he suggested they sit down. He led her to the couch where they sat together. She did not resist when he sat close to her. She leaned against him and held onto his hand. Finally he spoke.

"Cathy, I want to spend as much time as I can with you."

She released his hand to reach around and hug him tightly. When she raised her head his mouth came down to kiss her tenderly. The feeling was so soothing and heart wrenching that she made the first step a second time. Cathy felt as if her heart had leaped to her mouth with the sweetness of his kisses.

Finally she admitted to him. "Luke, I think I'm falling in love with you. Sometimes that scares me, but, whatever is happening, these creepy things, scare me even more. I just don't know what I can do."

He sighed then spoke. "Cathy, I love you, too. You don't know how much I want to share my heart and soul with you and how much I want you to know Jesus as I do. But that has to be your own choice. I can't make it for you. I just hope it is me and you are not just reacting to the love of Jesus in me." He nodded at her questioning look. Then he continued. "I know you don't understand, and these creepy things that keep happening don't help. Maybe God is using them to throw us together, I don't know. Right now I want to be with you as much as possible. I am praying for God to send his guardian angels to watch over you always."

"Do you really believe that there are guardian angels?" She asked him.

"Oh yes, the Bible tells us so. Cathy, I think you should eat something. Do you want to go to the kitchen?"

"All right. I am thirsty. But let's go together. I'll make some coffee."

When Saturday arrived and Cathy had told Jess about the flowers, Jess had wanted to stay home from work the following week to keep Cathy company. But Cathy had explained that she would be all right and Jess didn't need to do that. Then Jess had expressed her desire for Cathy to come to church with her. She said that since Elsie picked her up anyway it would be really easy for Cathy to go too. Jess had told her how much she enjoyed Ella's companionship also. Since Cathy had the free time this week end there was no reason why she couldn't go. Secretly, Cathy had hoped Jess would ask her so she could use that as an excuse for going. But, when she saw Luke that same day, he had insisted that he would pick her up and they could go out to dinner afterward. Cathy assured him Jess would understand.

After the service, Elsie had invited everyone to the farm for a light supper before the evening service. Cathy had looked apprehensive about going to church twice in one day after hardly ever going in her life, but Elsie waved her concern away lightly. When they were all seated around the Helpers' large table, Elsie explained that they thanked God for the meal before beginning to eat. All, including Cathy, bowed heads while John delivered the blessing. While they were eating Elsie asked Cathy if she had enjoyed the morning service.

"Actually, I thought it a strange coincidence that the preacher spoke about guardian angels. Luke and I were talking about that a few days before."

"Oh, there's no coincidence about it." John assured her. "That's just God's way. He knows what is needed even before we do. His love for us is perfect. We ain't ready to understand perfect yit. We're still growin' and learnin'. It takes a life time for that."

John's son Jack added, "Dad always says that."

John stated. "That's because it is true."

Elsie added softly, "Amen."

"Why did she say that?" Cathy asked.

Luke explained. "It means, it is certain. It's sort of like agreeing with what is said about God"

Jess remarked as if gaining new understanding. "Oh."

Then Cathy commented. "This milk is delicious."

All the children agreed in unison.

Cathy smiled and nodded when Elsie offered her more. She felt so at home and at ease among this friendly group. She could see that Jess did also. She felt grateful to Luke for bringing her here to meet and get to know such loving people. She took a deep breath and expressed again her thanks and appreciation.

Once the meal was finished Elsie spoke. "Cathy and Luke, come into the parlor with me while the children take care of the dishes. I have a gift for you Cathy." Elsie went to her bedroom briefly to retrieve the box. She had wrapped it in yellow and white figured gift wrap. She handed it to Cathy. "Actually, Cathy, this is from Luke, John and me. We hope you will enjoy it."

Cathy looked from the box in her hands to the other two who were smiling. She began to tear open the paper. When she opened the box cover, she beheld a Bible in modern translation with her name printed in large letters on the front. She removed it from the box, setting the box down on the coffee table. She opened it to reveal that it was in giant print. "Oh my, it's beautiful." Cathy was genuinely surprised by such a caring gesture. "No one has ever given me anything with my name on it and I can read this print very easily. I really don't know what to say. Thank you so very much. I will read it." She promised. She had to give each one of them a hug. When John entered the room she also gave him a hug and thanked him.

He smiled and said, "Now, we expect you to bring that with you tonight for service. Just remember, readin' and talkin' are two different animals."

All laughed and went to gather the children and prepare to leave for church.

8. The Costume Party

Cathy and Luke walked outside the auditorium where they had just attended the opening of a popular play. Cathy's hand was tucked tightly inside his arm and she was chattering about how much she had enjoyed the evening. Luke gestured and they continued walking in spite of the crispness of the night air. They discussed the play, the weather and other light hearted subjects as they strolled leisurely along the sidewalks of the city.

Luke commented. "I love being outdoors. I could walk for hours. Are you cold, Cat?"

She shook her head. Then she agreed. "I like to walk too. I'm used to our New England weather you know."

"Uh ha. How about some ice cream?"

"Ice cream?" She repeated.

He pointed to a shop just down the block.

"Okay, sure. It is refreshing to be out and about just for fun. No pressure. Oh, Luke, I feel so good when I'm with you."

The crowd had quickly thinned once they had left the auditorium. Neither of them heeded a darkly dressed figure on the other side of the street who seemed to be keeping pace with them.

Luke pulled his arm free to put it around her shoulders as they entered the shop together. They walked toward the rear and sat in a booth for two away from the chill near the door. When the waitress came, both of them ordered ice cream and iced coffee to drink. They talked congenially while they enjoyed their snacks.

"You are coming to church tomorrow, Cathy?"

She nodded.

"Great. I'll pick you up and we can go to breakfast first, say about eight–thirty in the morning?"

"Yeah, I guess so. It will be a short night."

"Sleep fast."

Cathy gave him a questioning look.

He elaborated. "My grandfather used to say that. If you don't have much time to sleep, he'd say, sleep fast." He grinned at her chuckle. Then he made a suggestion. "You know, there is a party at the Helpers' farm at the end of October. It's a costume party. They have a long hay ride, there's music and dancing, plenty to eat and no alcohol. Want to come with me?"

She repeated. "A costume party? I don't know what to wear. It sounds like fun though. I'll have to schedule with Penny, the other answering service operator, if I can. I'll see."

"Great. I'll just have to remember to ask you in advance so we can do things together."

She nodded. Then she said, "I never thought I'd be going to church."

He gave her a quizzical look.

She added, "I mean, I just never thought I would ever want to do something like that. See what you do to me?"

His grin gave him a boyish look, Cathy thought, but there

was nothing boyish about this handsome man. She realized that she must be staring as she hardly heard him speak when he rose.

"Come on, Sweetheart, it's getting late. I guess we'd better get going. Morning will come fast."

Cathy also stood and looked at her watch. "Luke, technically it is already morning."

He nodded briefly and turned to go.

A couple of evenings later, they were back at Cathy's apartment having dinner, when Luke asked her about progress of the police investigation regarding the obscure calls and other events.

Cathy replied. "What investigation. No crime has been committed so nothing can be done yet."

Luke frowned. Then he asked, "Well, what about the dead flowers that were sent to you? Did the police find out anything about that?"

Cathy shrugged her shoulders. "Not really. The officer said that the clerk at the delivery company claimed he had left the front desk for a few minutes and found the box with cash payment left on the counter when he came back."

"That sounds strange." Luke assessed. "So that means nothing is being done, right?"

"That's right. No crime has been committed so they can't do anything about what has happened to me. The officer even gave me back the answering machine tapes." Cathy concluded.

Luke shook his head and took another bite of food.

Cathy agreed to his silent protest. "Yeah, I know it doesn't make any sense. Maybe the person who made those calls will just give up, I hope."

Luke looked up. "Still, be careful, Honey."

She nodded.

The telephone rang. She sighed and rose to answer it. "Lein's Answering Line. May I..."

She was interrupted by the caller. "Do you have any calls for me? This is Dr. Davis."

"No, none."

"Okay. By the way, I saw you at the play the other night. Good bye." He hung up.

Cathy told Luke that it was the dentist checking in.

"Yes, but what did he say to upset you this time?" Luke asked.

Cathy gave him a startled look. "Well, he said he saw me at the play the other evening."

Luke put a hand to his chin and appeared to be thinking.

The next week end Cathy was on call when she received a phone call from her friend Jess.

Jess told her, "I'm having company tomorrow, Cat. Want to come over?"

"I can't Jess. I shouldn't leave the phone when I am on call. You remember?"

"Yes." Jess answered. Then she asked, "Aren't you going to ask who my company is?"

"Okay, who is it, Jess?"

"The guys from the group home in Hanover."

Cathy asked, "You mean the staff worker is bringing the residents to see you?"

Jess explained further. "No. I mean the guys, you know, Jim, Sam and Dick are coming, the guys from the staff."

Cathy was concerned. "Is Miss Shelton or some of the

women coming too?"

"Nope."

"Jess, is that a wise decision?"

"It'll be okay, Cat. Don't worry about me."

Cathy was skeptical but she didn't voice her opinion further. Instead she asked, "What are you wearing to the Helpers' costume party, Jess?"

"I don't know yet."

Cathy replied. "Me either. I'll talk to you later, okay, Jess?"

"Yes. Bye Cat."

Luke had offered to take Cathy and Jess shopping for costumes and out to eat afterward. The event took place during the day on a Saturday.

Once they were in a store he asked them, "Do you two have any idea what you would like?"

Both women shook their heads. They started to walk slowly around the store gazing at different outfits on display. Finally Jess spoke.

"I think I would like to be Cinderella. Do they have that one?"

Cathy found a ball gown with shoes and a crown. Jess took it to the clerk to see if she could get it in her dress size. Cathy and Luke continued to search. When Cathy picked up a Wonder Woman costume Luke smiled at her.

She said, "Hardly." then put it back down. After a sigh she commented. "I always liked the Wizard of Oz, but I don't want to be Dorothy."

Luke finally confessed, "I was thinking about Zoro myself. I'm pretty good with a scalpel, but I don't know about a sword."

Cathy grinned. After a few more minutes of browsing Cathy

commented. "Luke, I was trying to think of something to do with animals for you. How about the Lone Ranger? He wore a mask over his eyes and he rode a horse. I actually remember the old TV series."

It was Luke's turn to grin. After thinking a moment he agreed. "Not bad. Of course I can't come ridin' in on my Silver steed. I can ask. Now, what about you my pretty princess?"

She saw the twinkle in his eyes and felt her cheeks begin to color. She looked away, pretending to concentrate on the costumes, but not really focusing her attention on them. No one had ever used such terms of endearment toward her as Luke did. So intent was she on her own thoughts and feelings, she hadn't realized Luke had left until he touched her arm.

"Cathy, I've got it. You said you like the Wizard of Oz. How about a Glinda costume, you know, the good witch of the North? I asked when I went to see about mine and they both can be ordered to fit like Jess'es. What do you think?"

Cathy was nodding and smiling. Then she said, "Sure. I didn't even think of that. I'm going to feel like Cinderella at the ball though. I've never been to a costume party."

"Me too." Jess agreed. "I can't wait until we get the costumes so we can try them on. Oh, it will be so much fun. I am going to get a wig and shoes with mine. The lady said my shoes will look like they are glass slippers. I can't wait to see them."

Luke spoke as they walked outside. "I am glad you ladies are happy. John and Elsie are wonderful hosts. You will enjoy it. But, Jess, you aren't supposed to tell anyone who you are. That is the fun of costume parties. Everyone has a secret identity so you don't know who the person in the costume really is."

Jess exclaimed. "Oh I like that."

Cathy reiterated her pleasure. "It will be wonderful. I hope someone will take pictures."

Luke assured her. "Yes and video. John has lots of Helpers."

When the threesome entered the apartment building, Max hailed them from the office. He got up from his chair to retrieve a package and handed it to Cathy saying, "This came for ya. It was delivered by one of those postal truck services."

"Oh no." Cathy murmured. She took the box and thanked him. There was no return address. Her name and address were typed on the label. They walked Jess to her apartment then Luke escorted Cathy back to hers. Once inside she asked him.

"Luke, you will stay awhile won't you?"

He nodded. Then he asked her. "What's wrong, Honey?"

"I am almost afraid to open this. I haven't been receiving very good gifts lately. No return address. Luke you..."

He interrupted quickly. "Of course not. You know I wouldn't send you something without you knowing it was from me."

She nodded. "I know. Maybe it was just wishful thinking. Well, I guess I better open it and get it over with. I'll get a knife." They went to the kitchen together. Once she had opened the cardboard she first exclaimed then gasped. She removed a stuffed black cat from the tissue wrapping inside. It was lying face down in the box. When she turned it over there were two stuffing holes where the eyes had been cut out. "Why?" The word was a whisper. "This would have been so pretty." She sighed, set the stuffed animal down on the table and sat on a chair.

Luke picked up the box to further examine it. He picked two small button like objects from the bottom of the tissue paper. "Cathy, here are the eyes. Maybe they just fell off?"

Cathy put her hand over her mouth and shook her head. Finally she spoke. "No, they must have been deliberately cut out. Don't you see? Why is someone doing these things to me? I don't understand, Luke, I don't."

He put the box back on the table and pulled another chair next to hers. He sat and reached for her. She settled against him quivering slightly. "Sweet Cathy." He murmured softly. "You don't deserve any of this." After a time he spoke again. "I'm going to at least call the delivery company."

When he came back to the table she answered it for him.

"Same scenario, right? It was left on the counter with a cash payment. No one saw who left it."

Luke nodded and sat down again. He lightly kissed her forehead. Then he suggested to her. "You know, Elsie Helper could sew these back on for you and make it pretty again."

"Let's call her, Luke. Do you think we could go visit them now? Please, please don't send me any gifts, Luke, promise me. Not even a card, okay?"

"I won't send anything. I'll bring it in person. Do you want me to call?"

Cathy nodded and he rose to dial the phone number.

Elsie was more than happy to fix Cathy's gift. They spent a refreshing afternoon at the Helper's farm. Cathy cuddled the multicolored cat Missy on her lap while they talked at the kitchen table. Elsie had remarked when she had finished sewing, "There, it's as good as new. No one will ever know how it needed repair. You know, God is like that. He can easily repair broken lives and keep us in His watch care. We just have to trust Him."

"That's a tall order." Cathy stated.

John came into the kitchen just then. Everyone greeted him

cheerfully.

Cathy was grateful for the diversion. She hoped John wouldn't pursue the matter. She still felt uncomfortable on the subject of trust even though she had come a long way in revealing her feelings for her handsome beau. The remainder of the visit passed cheerfully and quickly.

When Cathy had free week ends she would attend church with Luke and the others every Sunday. She did occasionally read in her new Bible as she had promised. Her business was steady and she was thankful for that. If only these strange happenings could be solved her life would be doing very well. One Wednesday afternoon the door bell sounded. Cathy went to ask who was there. A male voice responded with the news of a package delivery for Miss Lein. Disgust and dread mingled as she reluctantly opened the door a little way. The delivery man handed her a vase of flowers, roses and violets. This time there was a card. She thanked him and closed and relocked the door. She took the card off and set the vase down on the coffee table. The card read:

Roses are red,

Violets are blue,

A surprise is coming

From someone you knew.

The card was unsigned. Cathy sighed and shook her head. She took the vase into the kitchen to water the flowers and placed it on the kitchen table. At least these were real flowers and not wilted or dead, but what of the message? Should she take it to the police? No, they couldn't do anything anyway and it didn't seem to be a threat in itself. Should she take it to Luke?

This was a church night. She went to look at a clock. She could get a bus and be there before the vet office closed. Cathy hurried to get her purse and heavy coat. She put the note into her coat pocket and left.

The veterinarian's office was busy when she arrived. She greeted the receptionist pleasantly and received a warm greeting in return. She didn't mind waiting and she understood that Luke was very busy today. Cathy went to take a seat.

"Hello, Cathy."

Startled, Cathy looked up to see who had spoken to her. A middle aged man holding a leash which was attached to a black and brown dog, who appeared to have no tail and a sleek smooth coat, had addressed her. She recognized him from the group Bible studies.

She replied in a cordial greeting.

The man continued. "I'm Ryan Sykes, a deacon at church. We met at the Bible studies at your apartment a couple of times. This is my Doberman Rusty. He's getting his annual check up."

Cathy nodded and smiled.

Lucy Becker stepped into the waiting room briefly to announce, "Rusty Sykes, you may come in now." Lucy must have seen Cathy but she made no indication of it. She shut the door behind the man and his dog.

Cathy waited while other patients were seen one at a time. It was after five o'clock when Luke finally came out. "Cathy, I'm sorry to keep you waiting so long. We had a lot of patients today."

"That's all right, Luke. I just wanted to show you this. I got some real flowers today and this card came with them. The person who ordered them paid cash so no info. was given to me about the order. See, it isn't signed."

Luke nodded. Then he offered to give her a ride home which she accepted. He had offered to stay with her instead of going to church service that evening but she had insisted it would be fine for him to go. She promised to call him there if anything happened. Nothing did.

When the date arrived for the costume party at the Helpers' farm, Cathy had forgotten about the anonymous card. She was so pleased with her costume, she had been looking forward to the event for such a long time it seemed, as did Jess.

The hay ride by horse and wagon provided John, who drove the two horse team, an opportunity to give a tour of the farmland. The ride was slow and bumpy but no one minded that. The view was breathtaking and, in spite of the crisp autumn air, the sun was shining brightly with few white puffy clouds in the sky. The hay wagon was full to almost over flowing. People sat on side seats, on the floor and some on the side and back rails. Everyone was talking and laughing. There was even a short time of sing along gayly led by John.

Cathy, who was experiencing hay for the first time, was surprised how prickly it felt, although she liked its sweet aroma. Luke was close with his arm around her as they traveled. She leaned even closer to her beau to speak softly into his ear. "Luke, this is such a wonderful experience, I want to thank God for this day."

He squeezed her shoulder a little in response. Then he replied. "You just did, Honey."

"What?"

He chuckled a little. Then he told her, "You just did thank God. You said it to Him."

"Really? It was...that easy?"

He nodded.

When the ride was over everyone jumped out of the wagon in turn. Once all were back on the ground they thanked John in unison and cheered and clapped. John acknowledged with a nod and a wave, then he patted his two team horses. His son Jack came to assist him with unharnessing and caring for the horses. The rest of the party had been invited to take part in several games at their own preferences. Time passed quickly. As twilight approached, it was time to change into costumes for the dinner and dance. Luke had explained to Cathy and Jess that once twilight began to creep in, people would know to slip away in order to go change, hopefully unnoticed by the majority of the other guests as the games continued, so that no one would know who anyone was under the costume. The surprise element would add to the fun as people would be revealed at the end of the evening. Everyone would try to guess who was under the costume as each one was unmasked. The person who got the most correct guesses would be declared the king or queen of the ball for that year. The previous years monarch had the honor of making announcements during the dinner and hosting the final event. There was always such a large turn out, from young to old, that it was virtually impossible for any one person to know every one. Elsie and John always told people they knew to bring others. Luke had also explained that the church assisted with the food and decorations since the annual event had become so popular in the town.

When prompted by her mother to go and change, Ella went to get Jess and took her with her to change in Ella's room. Ella told Jess that it would be alright that the two of them knew each other, but it would be their secret. Of course, Cathy, Luke and Elsie also knew Jess'es costume, but they wouldn't say anything. There might be more than one Cinderella or fairy princess there anyway. John had decided to be Tonto, the Lone Ranger's side kick. His son Jack had decided on Peter Pan. Elsie was dressed as the Queen of the May.

Luke had been planning how he would be able to separate himself from Cathy without her realizing it. It would be good for her to mingle with other guests as well. He pointed and led her toward a game of nurf ball. He explained what was being played and introduced her to the people who were not as yet wearing costumes. With a little encouragement and friendly greetings she started to join in the fun. A few minutes later when she turned around Luke was nowhere to be seen. She sighed and turned her attention back to the game. When the round had finished she thanked everyone and started to stroll leisurely around the grounds. A queen came near to her and took her hand. Cathy nodded and smiled. She knew it was Elsie who was leading her toward the house. Elsie let Cathy use her bedroom to change into her Glinda costume. Cathy again expressed her delight to her new friend who was just as pleased. Elsie loved people and enjoyed sharing time. This event had become very dear to her family. Cathy sensed a humble pride in the jubilant woman.

Smokey the Bear reminded everyone, "Only you can prevent forest fires." Then he began to grill hamburgers and hot dogs on the barbecue. Queens and princesses in ball gowns dressed and adorned large picnic tables with necessary supplies. The Seven Dwarfs ran around gathering up the children to bring them to the tables to eat. These were Elsie's and John's foster children who performed this task each year for their contribution to being helpful. Smokey was assisted by other animals in the cooking duties. Steamed corn on the cob, greens, beans, salads, cole slaw and gallons of iced tea, lemonade and water were in abundance. Breads and pastries served as desserts, as well as marshmallow toasting. Hot coffee and hot chocolate were also available. The apple cider could be had either way.

During the dancing Cathy felt as if she was Cinderella. She danced with many partners, including her Lone Ranger. As she was twirled by Donald Duck, a new partner took her hand. She almost gasped when she saw a black cat gliding her around the dance area. Her eyes widened and she felt her face pale, but the dancer didn't seem to notice. The black cat did not speak to her, just continued to dance then held her close. Suddenly she was dipped backward then brought up and twirled outward. This time a gloved hand took hold of hers and she was relieved to find herself in the arms of her Lone Ranger once more.

She whispered hastily to him. "Don't let go. Did you see that?"

He nodded. "I hadn't seen any black cats tonight yet, but I really wasn't lookin' for any."

"I hadn't either. Are you saying there could be more than one?"

"Could be. I've seen several fairy princesses and some other popular characters."

"Maybe it's alright then?"

"We'll try to keep an eye on it anyway. I'll alert John. Don't worry. I won't be gone long."

Elsie had won the contest the previous year and finally she

announced it was time for the finale, the guessing of each person present. "Since we have several Prince Charmings, I designate they shall be our official score keepers and their identities will be the last to be revealed. Now, as always, we will start with the youngest guest and children first."

Everyone had crowded into a large aisle way in the longest barn as the evening air was becoming nippy. The process went quickly amid exclamations of surprise and cheering when each person was revealed. Superman flew down from the hay loft on a wire to everyone's delight. He was revealed to be Ryan Sykes, one of the church deacons. Peter Pan also entered the same way. Applause and cheers ensued when Jack Helper was revealed. Horse hooves pounded on the ground two steeds stopped in one entrance way to the long barn. The two mounts descended and tied their horses to fence fails then walked together into the area. The Lone Ranger and Tonto were revealed to be Lucas Hoffman and John Helper who received much applause and loud cheering. Finally it came time to reveal the black cat. Cathy's heart pounded furiously at her memory. She had no idea if this person was the same one she had seen, but she couldn't help her nervousness. When the mask came off she gasped with recognition. It was Jim Ashton.

9. Mistaken Identity

Later, while the Helpers were busy bidding good byes to many of the guests, Cathy had an opportunity to introduce Luke to Jim. The three of them were standing in the parlor by themselves for the moment.

Jim had folded his arms across his chest and asked her, "Well, Cat, did you get my flowers? I wanted to surprise you."

Her breath caught. "Which ones?" She retorted with an edge to her voice.

Jim made a sniffling sound. "Oh, you have that many admirers? The roses and violets of course with the poem. Don't you remember?" He quoted the short verse. Then he added, "I wanted to surprise you, but I didn't expect you to be angry. What's up, Cat?"

"How long have you been here, Jim, in Manchester, I mean?"

Jim unfolded his arms and shrugged his shoulders. "I've visited a few times and Jess invited us to this party. I thought it would be a good idea. I thought we might try to get together again for old times." He shrugged his shoulders again.

Cathy was shaking her head. "I don't think so, Jim."

Jim gave Luke a scowl. Then he said. "I guess not."

Finally Luke spoke. "Jim, have you sent Cathy any other gifts?"

The other man shook his head.

Cathy asked, "Are you sure, Jim, no pranks?"

"What are you talking about, Cathy?"

She replied quickly. "Never mind. You could have signed the card though."

"Then it wouldn't have been a surprise."

Cathy was becoming frustrated by her circumstances. She really didn't know whether to believe her old boyfriend or not. Was it really a case of mistaken identity? Was he truly ignorant to her former circumstances? It made sense to her, and to Luke, that he could be harassing her out of spite or be trying to gain back the ground he had once had with her toward a renewed relationship. Either way, he was apparently back in her life again, and Jess'es.

Cathy had just gotten settled into bed one Saturday evening when there came a loud knocking on her apartment door. She got up to go answer it. "Who is there?" She called.

"Cat, it's me, Jess."

Cathy quickly unlocked the door and let her friend in. Jess was rubbing the back of her head as she went to sit on the sofa.

"Jess, what's wrong?"

"I was in the wash room washing my clothes for church tomorrow and one of the ironing boards on the wall came down and hit me in the back of my head. It still hurts."

Cathy examined it. It was already beginning to swell. "Oh, Jess, was anyone else with you?"

"No."

"Come on. I'll go back to your apartment with you. I'll fix an ice pack to put on that for you. Just let me get my key."

Once Cathy had seen Jess safely back into her own bed and gotten Jess'es clothes from the laundry room dryer, Cathy went back to her own bed. She was anxious to talk to Luke but did not call to wake him. She could discuss her thoughts with him after church in the morning. She sighed as she settled under her covers. She didn't think Jim's explanation had been entirely truthful and she didn't think this incident in the laundry room was merely an accident. Jim had known what her favorite color was. He knew some of her habits and preferences. She shivered even though she was snug under her bed covers. Why? She wondered. She had never done anything mean to anyone. She couldn't help her feelings of apprehension and her lack of trust with most people. Oh, please, she prayed unconsciously, don't let Luke betray my trust in him. Surely he couldn't be the one doing these things to her? Her sleep was fitful and restless. She was tired and moody the next day in spite of the pleasant weather and the pleasing companionship of her friends.

Cathy and Tina got together at Cathy's apartment that Monday morning. Cathy was grateful for the diversion. They were sitting at the kitchen table having coffee and talking following a short Bible study.

Cathy remarked. "I never thought I'd be studying the Bible."

Tina nodded. "Yeah I've said the same thing. Wasn't that party at the Helpers' great fun?"

Cathy nodded. "I never thought I'd enjoy being in the country either. I guess I've learned a lot of things since moving here."

Tina agreed. "Country life is certainly a change from the city though. I still like the city better, but that day was really fun. Oh, speaking of fun, I have a new guy who seems to enjoy having fun too." Tina smiled happily.

"Oh?" Cathy prompted her to continue.

Eagerly Tina obliged. "Yeah, we've gone out a couple of times. He seems to like dancing and having a good time. His name's Jim Ashton."

Cathy set her coffee cup down and put her hands in her lap. She felt her face get hot then pale. She could not hide her surprise. She had to say something. "Tina, I dated him a few times, in the past. We used to work together at a group home in Hanover."

Tina nodded. "Yes, I know. He mentioned that he knew you. That's what made me decide to go out with him in the first place. I didn't know him you see."

"Oh." Cathy didn't know exactly how to approach this subject. She hadn't felt so amiable about him once she had brought him to her apartment. Finally she asked, "Has he been to your place yet, Tina?"

Tina shook her head.

"Well, you might want to be careful about that."

Tina raised her eye brows. "What do you mean?"

Cathy sighed. "Well, he can be...very...forward. Just be careful, okay?"

Tina shrugged her shoulders. "Well, I guess you didn't get along very well with him then?"

Cathy shook her head. "Just be careful, Tina, and be aware of your surroundings."

"Okay. Well, this has been interesting, but I have to be going. We'll get together again, Cathy."

Cathy nodded and stood to walk Tina to the door.

Afterward she went back to take care of the dishes. She worked automatically, not really concentrating on what she was doing. Cathy wondered if she had been too revealing with Tina, but she didn't want the other woman to experience any of the things that she had been subjected to. She didn't know if her suspicions of Jim were real or not, but she felt she had to warn the other young woman at least. It couldn't hurt to be safe. Was she safe now? Would the weird pranks stop? She hoped so but didn't really believe they would. What could she do?

She jumped when the phone rang. She answered. To her relief it was a call for one of the doctors who was at lunch. She wrote down the information and said it would be relayed. Then she called the doctor's pager number. When he called her she relayed the necessary information cheerfully. He thanked her and hung up. She was relieved that this was an ordinary call. Her day progressed without incident.

When Luke arrived that evening she told him she felt like walking.

Luke asked. "Can you leave the phone?"

"It should be alright for a short walk. I'm just restless."

He took her hand as they left the apartment. On their way out of the building they saw Max sitting in the manager's office and waved. He nodded shortly as they passed.

Once outside Luke commented. "He must see a lot that goes on in the building."

Cathy shrugged her shoulders. "I guess so. Why?"

Luke replied. "Maybe I'll ask him to watch for anything unusual he might notice. Maybe he can be sort of a watch dog for the place."

Cathy smiled but she still held tightly to Luke's hand.

Then he asked her, "Are you feeling better today, Love?"

"I guess so. Things have been normal so far today. Luke, Tina is dating Jim."

"Oh?"

"Yeah, I was kind of surprised to hear that. I mean, I have been so apprehensive about him since...you know."

Luke nodded.

Cathy continued. "I told her to be careful."

Luke agreed. "Right. It is always best to be safe."

As they were passing the alley Cathy looked down that way. She stopped abruptly almost bumping into Luke. The alley was dimly lit as buildings obscured the street lights. She pointed.

Luke peered in that direction. He blinked trying to see in the dim light. Finally he whispered to her. "What is it?"

"I think it was the black cat like person. Didn't you see it?"

"I think I saw a shadow, but that was all." Luke responded. "Are you sure, Cathy?"

"I...I don't know. I only saw it for a second. Come on, let's get back. I don't want to be outside any more. It's getting chilly anyway." She looked away.

Luke put his arm around her waist and she did the same as they quickened their pace. Cathy kept looking over her shoulder but she saw no one. Once they were back inside her apartment she remarked. "I suppose you think I imagined it, don't you?"

"No, Cathy. Not at all. I just didn't see it myself. I just wondered if your imagination might be playin' tricks on you. Ya know, makin' you see something that wasn't actually really..."

She interrupted him. "You mean mistaken identity? Fabrication? I don't think so. I saw it move. Didn't you?"

"Well, it happened so quickly, I think I saw a shadow move

away, but I just caught a glimpse of whatever it was. Don't get upset, Darlin'."

Cathy sighed. "Well there was something there, wasn't there?"

He nodded. Luke went to sit on the couch and patted the cushion beside him.

She remained standing, looking thoughtful. "Luke, will you do something for me?"

He looked up.

"Go look on the fire escape outside my bedroom window?"

He rose to do so. When he returned he said, "There isn't anything there, Honey."

This time she came to sit beside him. "Okay."

10. Seeking Solace

Time seemed to pass slowly as winter set in. Cathy's business was steady. Emergency calls seemed to be on the rise with the seasonal change. In spite of the cold and sometimes treacherous conditions, Cathy still loved the snow.

During one of their morning studies, Tina told Cathy that she was going to host a Bible study gathering at her apartment on a Thursday evening.

Cathy smiled and then spoke. "See, now wasn't that easy?"

Tina nodded. Then she asked, "You are coming aren't you, Cathy?"

Cathy thought momentarily then answered. "I don't know if I can. I've been getting a lot more calls after hours with the winter weather."

"Oh. Well, why don't you see if the other lady can cover for you for a couple of hours that night?"

Cathy agreed. "That's a good idea. I'll call and ask her." She sipped her coffee.

Then Tina commented. "Hey, ya know Jim has been asking me about you."

"Really?"

Tina nodded. "Ya, he wanted to know if I knew anything about some pranks being played on you or something. I said no I didn't. Is something wrong?"

Cathy shook her head quickly. She didn't want to involve anyone else in her problems. No, it's just something we disagreed about the night of the costume party." She waved a dismissing hand. "Nothing important."

"Okay." Tina said. "I hope you can come to the study. I don't know what John will be talking on, I just said they could have it at my place like you did."

Cathy nodded. "Yes, John really makes it interesting doesn't he?"

Tina agreed. Then she thanked Cathy for the visit and got ready to go. As Tina was leaving the phone rang. Following the business call Cathy went to relock her door. As she did so she saw a delivery man approaching in the hall. She sighed and he spoke to her.

"Excuse me, ma'am."

She looked at him with a serious expression on her face.

"I have a delivery for Miss Cathy Lein. Is that you? This is the apartment number."

Cathy nodded silently and reached for the package.

"Thank you, ma'am." The young man said and turned to go.

"Excuse me." Cathy spoke finally. "Do you know who sent this? There is no return address."

"No, ma'am. I just drive the truck. You can call in though."

"Yeah, thank you." Cathy closed and relocked her door. "Not again," she said to herself. She took the box to the kitchen to open it. Inside she found a box of chocolates and there was a card. There was a typed message:

Pretty Cathy don't you worry.
Put aside all anger and fury.
Not a doubt should remain.
No I am not your enemy.

This time it was signed. Jim. Cathy opened her mouth in surprise. Was this evidence? Had Jim been the one sending the threatening messages all along? No. He wouldn't sign this if he had been doing that. She didn't know what to think. She resolved to show it to Luke when he came that evening. Cathy began to pace around the apartment restlessly. Her mind continued to work. What of Luke? Was she depending too much on him? She seemed to run to him every chance she could. Well, if they were in love with each other wasn't that natural? What if Luke was the prankster? The thought startled and scared her. She shook her head as if to banish the thought. No, he couldn't be. What was her mind doing to her? She needed something to occupy her mind. What had Luke told her? When he couldn't sleep he read a Psalm. Which one was it? She went to her bedroom and picked up her new Bible. She opened it to the book of Psalms and began to look through it. The table of contents told her that Psalm 119 was the longest one. She sat on her bed and began to read.

Later that afternoon Cathy received a call from Penny Jones asking if she could cover for the other woman on a Tuesday evening during the same week as the Bible study. Cathy assured her that she would and Penny agreed to take the evening of the Bible study. Penny had expressed her delight that Cathy was interested in that endeavor. Penny attended church as much as she could and she also enjoyed the women's group at her church. Was everyone a Christian except her, Cathy wondered. She still didn't understand the significance of it all.

After talking with Penny she felt somewhat relieved however. At least this time she had gotten a gift, although unwanted, that had a real person attached to it. She had calmed to a more pleasant mood as she prepared to bake chicken and potatoes for supper. After she had peeled and started the carrots cooking Cathy went down stairs to take her garbage bags out. When she came back inside she noticed that Max was still in the office. He appeared to be working hard, writing something, so she didn't speak, not wanting to disturb him. She hurried up stairs to her apartment.

The phone was ringing when she unlocked her door. She went to answer it. Her confidence boosted as it was another business call. By the time Luke arrived she was feeling happy and congenial. She had put on a pretty dress, he had remarked. He brought her a bouquet of bright red roses. She placed them at the center of the kitchen table and thanked him warmly. Then she told him about the gift with the card from Jim. Luke seemed to have a bewildered look upon receipt of this news.

He finally commented. "I guess I'll have to have a talk with that boy."

Cathy looked up from her pot of carrots. "Oh?"

He nodded. "Well, we can't have you receiving gifts from an old boyfriend now can we?"

"Really, Luke. He's hardly an old boyfriend. It was never a serious relationship."

"Does he know that?"

Cathy put her hands on her hips. "I certainly hope so."

Luke pulled out a chair and sat down at the table.

Cathy told him that the food would take a little while longer to cook.

Luke replied easily. "That's all right. There's no hurryin' something good. Come sit with me then." He took her hands when she did so. "Cathy, are you coming to the Bible study at Tina's next week?"

She nodded then told him. "Yes, I have it all arranged with Penny. She was happy about it. Luke, is everyone a Christian except me?"

He laughed a little then answered her. "Hardly. At least you are more open to the subject than when I first met you. Remember?"

She nodded. "Yeah, I know." She sighed. "I was trying to remember which Psalm you told me you read when you couldn't sleep at night. I was reading Psalm 119 today. It's the longest one I could find."

He squeezed her hands and nodded. "That's the one. Psalm 121 is also a great one for encouragement."

"You know so much about so many things, Luke."

"I wish I knew how to stop the creepy things that have happened to you, Cathy."

She nodded at his serious tone. "Maybe it is over now." She fervently wished this to be true but she really didn't think so. She got up to start the coffee perking.

Luke abruptly changed the subject. "You know, you should come home with me some week end to meet my folks up state. They have plenty of room now since two of my sisters are married. You can sleep in one of their rooms."

Cathy smiled at him and nodded. Time passed quickly as it always did when they were together. Cathy received a couple of business calls, but the evening passed without incident.

When the evening arrived for the Bible study at Tina's apartment, the focus of the discussion was depending on God for help. The reading was Psalm 121. Cathy had touched Luke's arm and he had just smiled and winked at her. Luke seemed to take most things in stride, except when it concerned Cathy. Tina, Cathy and Elsie had done some baking for the event. Refreshments afterward had been in abundance. Even though it had been after eleven o'clock once the gathering had disbursed, Luke went back to the apartment with Cathy for a few minutes alone with her.

He asked. "Did you enjoy the lesson tonight, Honey?"

She nodded and came to give him a light kiss.

His responding gesture was stronger and deeper. This time she did not resist. Then he murmured while cuddling her in his arms. He kissed her lightly again then spoke. "Cathy, it's getting harder to leave you each time I have to go."

She blinked and smiled a little then told him, "You'll just have to sleep fast, Love."

One mid morning when Cathy returned from errands, Max hailed her from the office. "Come in for coffee?" He asked.

She nodded and entered the office. She sat and thanked him for the hot brew.

"How are things?" Max asked as he sat back down.

She shrugged her shoulders.

"Your boyfriend told me about the strange things that have happened to ya."

"Oh, he did?"

Max nodded. "Sorry to hear. How well do you know that guy anyway?"

"Lucas, the veterinarian?" Cathy asked in surprise.

Max nodded.

"Pretty well. Why?"

"Just wondered." Max replied. "How do you know he isn't the one who is scaring you?"

Cathy set her empty cup down and shook her head.

Max added. "I just think you should suspect everyone. You want to be safe. I will keep an eye out for anything suspicious from now on."

"Thanks." She rose to leave.

When the time had arrived for Luke to leave for a week long convention, Cathy had almost forgotten he had told her about it previously. But she had made arrangements with Penny so that the other woman could have vacation time during Luke's absence. Cathy really didn't mind covering since Penny had been so cooperative with her. Luke had told Cathy that he really didn't want to leave her for so long a time, but the convention had been arranged before they had met. Cathy had assured him she would be alright. She promised she would call if need be. He had gone however reluctantly. Elsie Helper had also encouraged him that she would check in frequently with Cathy in his absence. Cathy smiled to herself. She had gained new and dear friends since moving here. As much as she loved Elsie, Cathy was still nervous about attending church without Luke. Even though she was on call, she had agreed to go to Sunday morning service, but not the prior Bible study session.

It was past eleven o'clock on Saturday night when she tramped down stairs to the laundry room to wash her clothes for the next day. She had put it off not wanting to leave the phone, but she knew she had to do it. She was feeling nervous and, she had to admit, fearful. Her stomach was churning. She didn't like being alone outside of her apartment at night. Jess was staying with Elsie for the week end and Tina was out on a date, probably with Jim. Her mind didn't want to dwell on that. Cathy didn't like always feeling fearful, but it was her nature. Hurriedly she started the washer and added her clothes. Once it was running she dashed back up stairs for the twenty minutes or so it would take to wash. All was quiet. She received no calls and there had been none on the answering machine when she had returned. She repeated the procedure when transferring the clothes to the dryer and went back to her own apartment. Once the dryer had finished she had to remain to fold them. Her breath caught as she heard a scuffling sound approaching the open door way.

"Well, hello, Cathy. I thought I saw a light on in here and came to check."

She let out a sigh. "Hello, Max. I'm just finishing up my laundry."

He nodded. Then he asked her. "Want to come over to my place for coffee?"

She shook her head quickly. "No, thank you, it is late and I am still on call. I just had to get this done tonight."

The man shrugged his shoulders and turned to scuffle away.

When her clothes were ready Cathy was relieved to turn off the light and go back up stairs.

The sermon the next morning was on trust. The pastor explained how Jesus had been betrayed by Judas and if we put our trust in human nature we are asking for betrayal or disappointment because human nature is not perfect. But if we are willing to trust God completely he is always faithful to forgive and accept us once we have trusted Him. Cathy remembered the quoted verse from 1 John 1:9. "If we confess our sins, He is faithful and righteous to forgive us our sins and to cleanse us from all unrighteousness."

Cathy also recalled Luke's favorite verse Proverbs 3:5–6. "Trust in the Lord with all your heart And do not lean on your own understanding. In all your ways acknowledge Him, And He will make your paths straight."

When Elsie brought her back to her apartment, Cathy thanked her and resolved to herself to go look up Luke's favorite verse in Proverbs. Again she was thinking of Luke. She shook her head. She knew she was depending too much on him. Her conscience still warned her to be careful, but her heart was singing a different song. Then she spent more time reading about Jesus in the Gospel accounts. Following that she read the letters of John.

That evening, when Luke had arrived and settled into his hotel room, he called her. She sounded happy when she told him of the church service that morning and her readings that day. Luke, encouraged by her animated conversation decided to take this opportunity to share.

"You know, Cathy, I didn't really understand what being a Christian meant until I was almost out of high school."

"Really? I thought you always grew up with that," she paused momentarily seeking how to phrase her question, then said, "mindset."

It was Luke's turn to hesitate. "Well, yeah. I mean, I did know, but knowin' and doin' aren't always the same."

Cathy sniffed. "Care to elaborate?"

"Well, I always knew that God existed. I could see a natural order in the way animals behaved that made sense to me. The seasons, growth of flowers and plants, and even the weather, although unpredictable, all seemed to have a balance that couldn't have just happened. But, I really didn't think much about it until I...got in trouble in school."

"What? You in trouble? I can't imagine that, Luke."

"Oh, yeah. I had some fights with other guys in high school...over games and girls." he quickly added before Cathy could ask. "Then, Dad had some serious talks with me about what I really believed and where I thought I was going with my attitude. It made me think, really look seriously at what Jesus was teaching. One Sunday afternoon I went fishing and our church pastor stopped by and talked with me right there on the shore of our pond. We had a long talk and I realized that I was no different than anyone else. But, if I really wanted to make a difference, in animals lives as well as humans, I would never be able to do it alone. Because we are human, and subject to sin, we can never make it on our own. It takes obedience to God and a willingness to let Him lead us to do things the right way. That is the only way things can work. His way truly is the best way."

"Yes, I am beginning to see that now, Luke."

"Wait. I have a verse." Luke pulled his pocket Bible open and paged through it until he found the scripture he was searching for. He read from Hebrews 11:28 NASB. "And we know that God causes all things to work together for good to those who love God, to those who are called according to His purpose." Finally he added. "Okay, that's my story."

"Wow." She breathed.

Their telephone time was as close as if they were sitting

together. She marveled within herself how comforting and reassuring their conversation was to her.

Luke, too, felt a sense of satisfaction as their conversation ended. Perhaps she is coming around to God's way, he thought to himself. He settled comfortably in bed and began to pray.

On Wednesday afternoon another delivery arrived for Cathy. Again there was no return address. She took the box to the kitchen to get a knife. She sighed and shook her head as she opened it. As the cardboard flipped back, something made a rattling sound and the top of the object popped up revealing the head of a black cat with white around the facial features, the eyes, nose and mouth. It was attached to a spring. The object was a jack-in-the-box. Cathy gasped and pulled it free from the cardboard box. She slammed the cover down to close it. Retrieving the discarded cardboard box from the floor, she found a folded piece of paper in the bottom. On it was typed a short verse.

Time's claws shred no memories.
Sickening pain haunts endlessly.
Again in vain I cry her name.
Each time silence fails to stop the pain.

Her eyes widened and she gasped when she saw, under the verse, the typed name Luke. The paper dropped to the table top as Cathy sank into a chair. Her senses felt numb. She couldn't think. It just couldn't be true...could it? Was Max right? Had it been Luke all along? Bible verses mixed with the verses so ingrained in her mind now. Her throat tightened but tears would not come. She just felt so dull, like there was no feeling at all left in her. She did not even heed the phone when it rang. She did not know how long she sat at the table, but she knew she had been depending too much on Luke. The Bible was right, you couldn't trust any person, not completely.

She was alone.

11. Love Regained

Cathy avoided calling Luke back for the remainder of his absence. She could not bring herself to talk to him over the phone. She didn't return Elsie's calls either, or any of her new friends, except Jess. She had to talk to Jess or the other woman would be knocking at her door demanding to know what was wrong. Cathy finally told her friend that she didn't feel well and just wanted some time alone to recover. It wasn't a lie after all.

Luke had taken the earliest possible flight back and didn't even bother to unpack. He threw his suitcase and briefcase into his apartment and closed and relocked the door, then he went to Cathy's. He knocked loudly and called to her. "Cathy, it's Luke. Please let me talk to you."

Her heart pounded as she went to the door. She had tried to mentally prepare for this day of reckoning, but all guards and plans scattered now. Her stomach was so knotted it was cramping violently. She said nothing as she let him in and relocked the door.

"Cathy, are you all right? What is wrong?"

Silently she went to the closet in the living room to retrieve the latest gift. She handed the box to him. Once he had opened, then closed it, she handed him the typed note.

As he sat down in a chair his face paled then turned red with anger. He looked up at her still standing in front of him. "Cathy, surely you know I didn't. I couldn't. Truly I didn't, Love. I had no idea of such a hateful thing. Cathy?"

She sighed. "What did you expect me to think?"

"This is why you wouldn't talk to me. Oh, God, how, why? Who could have done this terrible thing and for what earthly reason? Cathy, I love you. I would never hurt you like this. Please."

She finally sat and propped an elbow onto the side of the couch arm. She rested her chin in her hand. Finally she spoke. "I guess I knew you didn't, but it was very upsetting when I got it. It took me days to get over this. I got it on Wednesday afternoon. I just couldn't deal with it right then."

"Oh my Darling Cathy. I know the Lord says vengeance is mine, but I would like to get my hands on whoever is doing these awful things." Luke vowed. He rose and began to pace the floor. Finally he hit the wall with his fist. Cathy jumped at the gesture. She had not seen him really angry before. Luke sighed and apologized. "I'm sorry. It just makes me so angry inside. Cathy I love you, you must know that."

She nodded her head slowly. Then she asked, "What can we do about these things? I was just beginning to get comfortable with reading the Bible. I even remembered some of the verses you liked. It always happens. When I begin to get comfortable something bad happens to spoil it. I guess I'm not meant to be happy."

Luke shook his head and came to sit beside her. "No, my love, don't even think that. Cathy..." Luke leaned toward her but she did not respond. He stopped and sat looking at her.

"Luke, I can't trust you that much, I mean, I shouldn't depend on you that way. Please don't, not right now."

He sighed and nodded silently. "Can we at least still see each other, date each other?"

She nodded.

"All right. Do you want me to leave?"

She shrugged her shoulders then replied. "I don't know."

Then he asked her. "Can I pick you up for church tomorrow morning?"

"Yes that will be okay. I guess I'll have to talk to Elsie. I've been avoiding people since..."

He could see the pain in her eyes still fresh.

"Luke."

"Yes, Cat."

She blinked at the affectionate tone to his voice as he used her pet name. "Please, don't send me any gifts."

"No, Sweetheart, I have already promised you. I haven't and I won't. I'll pick you up about eight thirty in the morning. Good night, Love."

Following service Elsie had persuaded Cathy and Luke to come to visit at the farm. Cathy was reluctant but she knew she had to make amends. Penny had returned from her family vacation also the previous day and she had offered to cover for Cathy today. Cathy was grateful and received the offer with thanksgiving. She felt safe at the Helpers' farm. They were talking congenially at the kitchen table while the children were outside playing. Ella and Jess were watching a movie in Ella's room. Everyone had skirted around the subject of Cathy's behavior the past half week.

Finally Cathy opened up and talked about the delicate situation she found herself in.

Once Cathy had explained her latest gift and the typed note Elsie exclaimed. "How awful! I can't even imagine something like that. No wonder you were ill over it. Did you call the police?"

Cathy nodded. "Yes, but the only prints on the thing were mine and Luke's."

Luke hastened to add. "She called them yesterday after I got back. I had already touched it before the policeman came. I say again, I never sent her anything after the first bouquet of yellow roses. She had asked me not to and I wouldn't break a promise."

Elsie reached out to pat his hand. "Of course you wouldn't, Dear."

Then John spoke. "There must be some way to stop this nonsense. Maybe the delivery companies need more security. Somebody is bound to see something if they just look for it."

Luke looked at his friend. "John, that's it. Maybe nobody is looking hard enough. Maybe we need to be our own detectives. We can be aware and alert ourselves. Maybe we can solve this terrible thing."

Elsie was shaking her head. "Now you boys need to be careful. I think we had better pray."

Everyone, including Cathy, joined hands and bowed heads to petition for Cathy's safety.

Afterward Cathy confessed. "Thank you, all of you, I do feel better now."

Although she was feeling more herself, Cathy still tried to keep her relationship with Luke casually friendly. He made no advances toward her although he still used his affectionate terms. She allowed him that. She realized that she couldn't trust anyone, not completely. She knew trust was a big step. She did not offer this lightly. But, what about Jesus. He had made the ultimate sacrifice for us, mere humans. Was there real truth to the words in the Bible? She continued to wonder. Unconsciously she was recalling more Bible verses as her thoughts tumbled. The words of one of Luke's favorite verses repeated itself in her mind, Proverbs 3:5. 'Trust in the Lord with all your heart And do not lean on your own understanding.' She had much time for reflection as she had to spend so much of her time at home. She still saw Luke regularly though. She could not stop her pleasurable thoughts of him from creeping into her consciousness.

On one of her free Saturdays he had taken her out for the day to a country fair. She was able to forget her troubles and truly enjoy the day. When they returned to her apartment late that evening she arranged the new stuffed animals he had won for her around her living room. She took a couple of her favorites to her bed to rest there. These were cats. Then they went to sit on the couch together. She was smiling.

Cathy commented happily. "What a truly beautiful day. I will treasure it always, Luke."

He grinned then spoke. "'A joyful heart makes a cheerful face,'"

She laughed. "Okay, is that from Proverbs?"

Luke nodded then finished the verse. "It's Proverbs 15:13. And here's the rest of it. 'But when the heart is sad, the spirit is broken.'"

Cathy pulled in her breath then reached for him. She was unable to stop herself. His expressiveness was so tender, so true. Her lips were on his with her heart in her mouth. His response was genuine and deep. She allowed him to hold her again. They both rested in the sweet silent solace of each other.

Luke silently thanked God for an answered prayer. He had longed to have this closeness back. He would treasure this moment of love lost and love regained.

At the close of church service the next morning, Luke had a dream come true. Cathy reached for his hand as she stood to go forward. He accompanied her as she received Jesus as her living Savior and took Him into her heart. God had taken something bad, the cat–in–the–box, and turned it into something good, her salvation. Luke knew that she had learned a valuable life lesson. Even though she was not able to trust even him completely, God would never fail her. He knew now that she knew the difference and her step was genuine. Luke, too, was crying with joy for her decision.

Such a monumental event called for celebration at the Helpers and then a return to service that evening. Cathy listened with new interest as she followed in her large print Bible. All too soon it was time for Luke to take her home. He expressed his reluctance at leaving her but she had assured him she would be fine now. As he left, Luke thanked God for Cathy's decision. Maybe now God could start putting things right in her life.

They were preparing to wash and dry dishes together one evening after supper at Cathy's apartment when Cathy began to question the awful events again. She had filled the sink with hot water and was beginning to wash. She spoke with frustration in her voice.

"Luke, I just don't understand how someone can keep getting away with these...pranks. How no one ever sees a package being left with no return address, always typed, always paying by cash, always..." She stopped and gasped.

"What's wrong, Honey?" Luke asked.

"Always knowing what is important to me...The dead flowers were yellow, which is my favorite color. The cats...with no eyes...the cat–in–the–box, even the note from you...supposedly. I got it on a Wednesday, Luke. That's the day you usually have church in the evening."

"Cathy." Alarm was evident in his voice too. He recalled that during the convention Tuesday evening was the last time he had spoken to her on the phone before he came back to confront her.

She began to scrub hard fast circles on the plate she was continuously washing. Cathy added. "Then there is that person by the alley." She splashed the water and looked at her beau. "Luke, someone is stalking me!"

12. Police Interrogation

The phrase hung over them for a time. Both had known but neither wanted to voice the haunting truth. Luke took the plate from the water, rinsed it and placed it in the dish strainer. Then he removed her hands from the water, dried them and led her to sit at the table.

Finally Cathy uttered the word. "Who?"

Luke sighed. "If you are being stalked, which makes sense, it has to be someone who knows a lot about you."

"Well, everyone at the group home knew my pet name, and Jim knew my favorite color. They knew I like cats too. Jim did send me a poem. Oh, Luke."

"We don't know for sure if it is Jim. He has denied it, you remember."

She nodded.

Luke asked. "Does anyone else know a lot about you...besides me?"

"I don't know really. I didn't think I was very open to people. But, I don't know now."

"Cathy, I think you should talk to the police again, at least try."

"I suppose so." She agreed. "I'll go tomorrow morning and get it over with. You better not come with me." She told him anticipating his response. "They may suspect you too."

He nodded his silent affirmation. Then he rose from his chair. "Let's get these dishes done."

Cathy had called prior to visiting the police station. As she had expected, the questions seemed as if she were being interrogated. She didn't know if she had any enemies. She believed she could trust Luke with her welfare. Her old boyfriend Jim showed no animosity toward her now. In fact, he had denied knowledge of previous incidents even though he had sent one of her gifts. Luke had sent her flowers only once and he adamantly denied sending the second box even though the note had his name typed on it. Cathy also explained how they were also concerned about her friend Jess because of the writing on the wall in the laundry room at their apartment building. She didn't know if Jess had any enemies. She didn't think so. Jess had moved here not long after she did.

"All right, Miss Lein, when did these pranks start?"

"What do you mean, when?" Cathy asked.

"I mean approximately during what time period. Was it after Jess moved here?"

"No. It was just prior to it. The first prank was on my answering machine. I can get the exact date and time from the tape. I saved it."

"Good." The officer replied. "Let's see if we can develop a time line, maybe establish a pattern."

Cathy nodded. She hadn't thought of that approach.

The officer was speaking again. "Try to recall as much detail as you can when something happens. Be aware of your surroundings and observant."

Again she nodded.

"Who knows that you are dating the veterinarian?"

"Most everyone I know now." Cathy admitted.

"Well, give me a list of your family and friends. That is a place to start."

Cathy obeyed and began to write. The officer had given her a notebook in order to keep a journal of happenings. When she had finished she handed the piece of paper that she had torn out to the officer. Then she explained. "There is no family. I think my friends Luke, Jess and the Helpers should be above suspicion."

"No one is above suspicion." The officer retorted.

"Oh, well, I am not doing these awful things to myself." Cathy replied.

He nodded shortly. Then he asked another question. "How many of your friends write poetry?"

"I didn't know any of them did."

"That isn't helpful, Miss Lein."

"Should I ask them? Luke says he's never written any."

"No, don't arouse suspicion." The officer told her.

"All right. Well, at least you believe me now?"

"We'll keep it open for investigation. That's it for now." He handed her a business card. "You can contact me if you need to."

"Count on it." Cathy then thanked him and got up to leave with the notebook and her purse.

Obediently Cathy went home and started her list describing the incidents with dates and times as best she could. She also included the accident Jess had in the laundry room. She remembered her own fearful evening there. The building manager had stopped in, but there was nothing significant about that. Should she include it? She did. Upon studying the list in front of her once it was completed she realized the significance of one of the detective's questions. When Luke arrived that evening she showed him her charted events. After allowing him to study it for a few minutes she remarked.

"Luke, someone even knows that we are dating. The last thing I got was on a Wednesday. That's the day you usually go to church instead of coming here. I wonder if whoever it is knew you would be away at the convention that week?"

Luke looked at her with a startled expression. "This is really getting scary, Cathy."

She nodded. "What can we do?"

He replied. "I don't know." After a moment he added. "Start praying unceasingly." Following a brief pause he asked, "Are the police going to be questioning people you know?"

She answered quickly. "No, they don't want to be conspicuous and scare whoever it is away. I'm supposed to be more alert and aware and write things down that are significant."

"That's it?"

"Pretty much for now." She told him.

"Oh, they can't do anything until...until it's too late." Luke said it with sarcasm.

Cathy came to put her hand on his arm. "Maybe God will help us now that I'm a new Christian."

Luke took her in his arms and cuddled her. He wanted to comfort, shield and protect her, but he knew not from whom. After a few moments of comforting silence, Luke spoke softly. "Cathy, promise me something."

She murmured.

"Don't go anywhere by yourself alone and that goes for Jess too."

"Luke, sometimes I just have to go pay bills or get something I forgot at the store. You know how that is."

"Yes, but you can't take any chances now. Remember Jess'es accident. Can't you use the same para transit transportation as Jess? I don't think you should be taking the public bus by yourself until this is solved. You've got to take more precautions. You have enough friends here now that you can get someone if you need to go out."

His kisses were soft and soothing. Cathy sighed and finally agreed. "Yes, I know. I understand what you are saying." Her arms around him tightened. "Oh, Luke, I am so happy to have you. I do love you dearly."

"Now you have me and Jesus who love you." His hands cupped her face as they both smiled.

She whispered to him. "The light of your eyes rejoices my heart, Love."

His arms came around her again in a tight embrace. Silently he prayed for God's protection and direction for their lives and their future.

13. See The Black Cat

As promised, Cathy went home with Luke for the Thanksgiving weekend. Jess had been invited to stay with the Helpers. Cathy got to meet Luke's youngest sister Roberta, who went by Bobbi, as well as his parents and grandparents, some uncles, aunts and cousins. Everyone was delighted to meet Cathy and Luke endured much teasing. He was happy to show her his high school, places he liked to hang out around town and the beautiful countryside. She had remarked how breath taking it all was under it's white snow covering. She was introduced to his pets and told him she would never be able to remember all of their names. She was surprised at how easily all of the animals seemed to warm up to her. Luke's mother had remarked that she must have a kind heart since the animals liked her. This was a very favorable sign she had told her son. Luke had also expressed his joy at Cathy's recent decision to follow Jesus. She showed her gift Bible to his parents who told her she had made a wise decision and would never regret that choice.

His mother had confided to Cathy that this was the first time he had brought a girl home since he had left for college. She also had thanked Cathy for enduring Bobbi's initiation challenges. Cathy had laughed and said she didn't mind. She loved the snow and being asked to go sledding and snow ball fighting were welcome exercises. She had not slid down such steep hills before though, but it was all right. She had enjoyed every heart stopping minute. Bobbi had insisted that the girls go alone, without Luke, at first. This was on Saturday morning. When the two had returned to the farm house Luke met them at the kitchen door as they entered.

"No broken bones?" He asked Cathy.

She laughed and shook her head.

Then Luke had looked at his sister and asked, "Well, did she pass?"

Bobbi was smiling and nodding. Then she said simply "Yup."

Luke sighed. "Good. Now we can all rest easy."

As she had sat down at the table once she had removed her snow gear, Cathy remarked. "Bobbi, you and my friend Jess would get along great. I hope you can meet her someday."

At Sunday morning church service the pastor had announced that Luke was back for a visit and had made Luke stand to be recognized so that everyone could greet him after service. Luke took it all in stride. His pleasure at being able to share his boyhood with Cathy was abundantly evident.

Following Sunday service, Luke's mother had insisted that they stay for dinner before driving back to Manchester. Cathy could feel the mixture of emotions that her man was feeling. She knew it was hard each time he had to leave such loving, caring family. She felt gratitude that he had shared so much of himself with her. His mother was preparing a lunch for them to take back. Cathy knew that if Luke shared even half of it with her she would have food for several days.

Cathy thanked each of his family, his parents, grandparents and Bobbi and received hugs from all of them. Luke's mother told her she would be welcome any time she wanted to visit, with, or without Luke. Cathy had laughed and thanked her sincerely for everything. Bobbi was also getting ready to go back to college as her father would drive her to Keene State. She also received the hugs and kisses from everyone, including Cathy. Bobbi and her father left about the same time as Luke and Cathy. It was after three in the afternoon. The sun would be setting within the hour. It would be dark when all had reached their destinations. Luke promised to call once they had gotten back safely. He and Cathy chatted happily and intimately as they drove.

Cathy remarked to him. "No wonder you are such a loving, caring person, Luke. Your family is beautiful, even Bobbi. Are your other two sisters like her?"

Luke chuckled a little. "Maria and Hilda are more sophisticated, but they have her spunk and spirit. I am so glad you enjoyed the visit, Honey. It meant a lot to me."

"Oh, Luke, it meant a lot to me too. You look a lot like both your parents. I have never met such caring people before I met you."

"Cathy, you know, as much as the Helpers and my folks are loving, Jesus loves us infinitely more. He laid down his life for all of us. Even before we were conceived, he loved each one of us."

She nodded silently. Finally she spoke. "Yes, I am beginning to understand that."

Luke smiled then said, "The more we experience the more

we realize how deep and awesome God's love is for us. Oh, Cathy, I will treasure this holiday week end always."

She moved closer to him and briefly rested her head on the edge of his shoulder.

Once back at her apartment Luke had helped her take some of her share of food to Jess. Cathy had told him she had more than enough and wanted to tell Jess about her week end while she had some free time. She had checked her machine and found no business calls since Penny was covering for her. Penny hadn't minded at all since their family Thanksgiving was going to be at her home this year. To Cathy's relief there was nothing out of the ordinary in her mail either, just bills. Luke had left her with Jess to catch up on the week end.

Cathy's spirit had been refreshed and renewed by her visit. She was able to settle back into the routine of her business with new strength and peace of mind. Luke spent as much of his free time with her as he could. Although she still did not go to church service midweek because of her business, she had agreed to host Bible studies at her apartment whenever the group needed a place. She attended Sunday service on alternate week ends as she shared the time with Penny.

A heavy snow one Friday morning, which had begun the previous evening, had prevented Jess from going to work that day. By afternoon the snow had tapered to light flurries. Jess had asked Cathy to go with her to the park for some snow time. Cathy happily agreed, but told her friend she had to get back around five o'clock to be available for the phone. Jess nodded her understanding.

Other children and young people had the same hardy spirit and were doing the same. The fresh snow was light and powdery so it had to be thrown in clumps for snow ball fighting. Jess liked to make tracks and then see if she could retrace her steps in the same prints. Sometimes she would fall as she had zig zagged her feet hurrying to set her tracks. Cathy laughed as they shared in the winter fun with the other residents of the neighborhood.

Cathy was tramping through the snow toward a snow covered bench to wipe it off to sit for awhile when she caught a glimpse of a dark figure behind some trees that would shade the bench when the sun was shining. She pushed her glasses up with her finger and stared. She saw dark clothing, like exercise clothes and a hood over the head. When the face turned toward her briefly she gasped as she could see clearly the cat mask. Cathy turned to run back to where Jess was scooping up some snow. Cathy called as she approached her friend.

"Jess, look over there by the park bench near the trees."

Jess looked up but she saw nothing.

"Jess, did you see it?"

Jess shook her head then asked "What, Cat.?"

Cathy's breath came hard and fast. "The black cat, did you see the black cat person?"

"No." Jess answered.

Cathy insisted. "It was right over there, behind the trees near the bench. I saw it."

Jess said. "Oh. Maybe it is gone now."

Cathy nodded but said nothing more. She looked closely at her watch. It was twenty minutes to five. Then she asked Jess if she wanted to go back inside.

"Oh, Cat, let's stay a few more minutes. Can we?"

"Okay." Cathy agreed.

Jess continued to play with the snow awhile longer. Cathy stood and watched. She also looked around but saw no one out of the ordinary now. Had her mind been playing tricks on her she wondered.

No, she thought. She had seen it. She knew what it looked like now.

When Luke arrived that evening she told him about the incident. He had been late as travel was difficult with plows out still trying to clear roadways.

Luke asked, "Did anyone else see it?"

Cathy shook her head.

"That's too bad."

Cathy agreed. "Yeah, I know. So you do believe me then?"

"Yes. Why wouldn't I?"

She sat next to him on the couch and leaned against him as he put his arm around her. "Thank you for that. I know I am not imagining it."

Luke asked, "Did you call the police?"

"No. It happened so quickly and so briefly. What could they do? I will write it down though. Thanks for reminding me." She got up to go get her notebook from the bedroom and wrote the details of the incident. Then she went to the kitchen to see about supper for them.

Luke had asked Cathy if she wanted to get a real tree for her apartment for the Christmas holiday. Since she was going home with him to his parents she didn't see the need to have one. Jess, however, had wanted to get a small one for her apartment even though she would be spending the holiday with the Helpers. Cathy replayed their conversation over in her thoughts.

"Why don't you want a tree?" Luke had asked.

She had merely shrugged and replied, "I just don't want to bother with it, Luke, since I'm going to your folks anyway."

Luke had made a puppy dog sad face at her. "Oh, Cat, I just love the smell of the fresh tree in the house. When you put the lights on and the decorations, it's so cheerful and bright. It would add warmth to your place. You spend a lot of time here anyway. Did you know that the Christmas tree is the symbol of eternity. It reminds me of God's promise of a better life to come in Heaven. I think it would make such a pretty picture in front of your window." He had pointed to the spot.

She smiled a little to herself as she absentmindedly wandered over to her living room window. Then he had pleaded.

"So what do you think...right here...how about it?"

She had gone to put her arms around him then. Quietly she admitted, "You know I can't resist you, Luke. Okay, we'll get a tree. Jess will be excited, I know."

She still remembered his kiss. That was the wonderful part.

One Saturday afternoon Luke took Cathy and Jess to a tree lot in his truck where they could pick out just the right tree. They would have to be small ones in order to transport both of them back. They walked around for a long time. Most of the trees were large and full. Finally Luke saw an area where there were several smaller ones and he pointed in the direction. When Jess found one that she liked he went with her to mark it to show the lot manager. Cathy was still looking around.

Luke turned as he heard Cathy hurriedly crunching through the snow toward them. She put a hand on his arm and pointed.

"Luke, I saw it again. I saw the black cat person. It was holding up an ax!"

14. Imagining

"Cathy, calm down." Luke told her. "Slow down and tell me where you saw it."

Cathy turned and pointed toward an area of tall trees. "It was over there. I just saw it for an instant. Luke, I really did see it."

"Okay. Let's walk that way." Luke suggested. "Maybe it's still around here." They walked around a bit but saw no one else.

Cathy stopped walking. "Why am I the only one who sees this thing? Luke I didn't imagine it."

Luke shook his head. "I don't know. We better get back to Jess. Are you going to the police?"

Cathy threw out her hands then slapped her sides. "I don't know. I'll write it down though when we get back. I don't understand this. You do believe me, don't you?" It sounded as if she were questioning herself.

Luke nodded silently.

Since Tina had the next Monday off she came to Cathy's that morning for their frequent short Bible study. Tina remarked that Cathy's tree was cute. Cathy, Luke and Jess had decorated her small but full tree that stood in her living room. It was in a corner that could be seen as soon as the door was opened. They sat in the living room to talk instead of in the kitchen following the study.

"I guess I'll have to get a tree too." Tina commented. "I didn't think I would since I don't spend a lot of time in my apartment."

"Oh?" Cathy asked.

Tina nodded. "I'm either working or out with Jim lately."

"How can you be out with Jim so much?" Cathy asked.

"Oh, didn't I tell you? Jim moved here to Manchester."

Tina noticed Cathy's surprised expression. Then she continued to explain.

"Yeah, he got a job here as a mechanic for a local garage. We've been going out a lot. We like a lot of the same activities. Besides, he's a lot of fun to be with. Hey, would you and Luke like to double with us sometime?"

Cathy had a bewildered expression on her face. After a thoughtful pause she replied. "I don't know. I'll ask Luke about it."

Tina nodded. "Okay. See you later. I've got to be going now."

After Tina had gone Cathy decided to call the detective who had given her the business card to make another appointment. Luckily he could see her that afternoon. She hurried to get ready and had to take the bus. There was not enough time to arrange for the para transit. They needed twenty–four hours notice to arrange a trip.

Following their talk Cathy decided to meet Luke at his office rather than going straight home. She knew he would give her a ride and she wouldn't have to pass that haunting alley on her way home. Besides, she enjoyed seeing his clients and some of their owners. She smiled pleasantly as she was cheerfully greeted by his receptionist. When the woman called back to tell Luke Cathy was there he immediately came out front.

Stepping over to her he asked, "Cathy, is everything all right?"

She nodded then answered him. "Yes. I just had an opportunity to talk with the detective this afternoon and took the bus here instead of going straight home. I hope you don't mind. I'll wait. I see you are busy as usual." She smiled a little.

Luke nodded and turned to go back into the examining room.

A little while later Lucy Becker came out to announce his next patient. "Tabatha Grayson, you may come in now." An older lady holding a black cat stood and picked up her carrying crate with the other hand to follow Lucy inside. Cathy silently admired the pets while waiting for the close of the business day. She could see that animals needed special care but she felt they could be wonderful companions also. A young man with red hair and glasses was holding a leash attached to a dog with reddish hair Cathy guessed to be an Irish setter. A middle aged man had a leash attached to a German shepherd Cathy recognized. Lucy Becker reappeared and announced "Barney Sawyer, you may come in now." Cathy was surprised when a petite blonde stood and began to coax a large brown and white St. Bernard to get up. Once the massive dog had risen, he obediently walked beside the small woman. Cathy had been wondering why the name of Tabatha Grayson had sounded familiar. Finally she realized that she had taken a call for Luke from a woman with a newly pregnant cat. She thought she would ask him about the patient she saw here today. It must have been the same cat. Cathy marveled at how innocent cats seemed to be to her. Yet, the cat like person represented something sinister, threatening, ominous, but it had never done anything but stare at her. It haunted her dreams. But she still loved cats no matter what color they were, even black ones.

"Cathy..."

Roused from her thoughts she looked up to see Luke standing in front of her. She must have dozed off or been day dreaming. All of the patients had gone. She and Luke were alone as she looked around the office.

"Oh, Luke, I must have been day dreaming. By the way, I wanted to ask you, was that woman Mrs. Grayson, the one who had called about her Tabatha being pregnant a few months ago?"

He was nodding. Then he explained. "Tabatha had a litter of eight kittens. All lived. The Graysons had to give them away. We have fixed that situation since then."

Cathy smiled. Then she asked, "Are you ready to go?"

"All set. Shall we pick up something to eat on the way back to your place?"

"Oh, I guess so." She agreed.

She followed him outside and waited for him to lock the door and set the security alarm before they left. When they had entered the apartment building with their pizza and soft drinks, they saw a light on in the laundry room. Luke suggested looking in to see who was there. When they did they were greeted by a verse written in red on the wall by the washers. No one else was present. Silently they each read the dreaded words.

A time of innocence no longer mine.
I remember another frail feline,
A woman's body with adolescent mind.
Her fate sealed by providence divine.

Cathy spoke first. "Oh, Luke, surely I'm not imagining this. What is going on here?"

"Wait here, will you? I'll go get Max and show this to him." Luke suggested.

Cathy protested. "Wait. Why don't you stay? I'll go. I don't want to be alone in here."

Luke nodded.

Several minutes later she returned with the building manager. "What in the world?" He was as surprised as they were. "That looks like blood." Max reached out with his finger.

Luke raised a hand. "Don't touch it. Will you call the police?"

Max nodded. "I'll take care of it." He turned to scuffle out.

Cathy and Luke took their belongings to her apartment. He had to coax her to eat.

Cathy made another appointment to talk to the police detective. This time she used the para transit service and planned for a half hour visit. Once she was seated she asked her first question.

"Can you take a sample of everyone's handwriting who lives in the building or something?"

The detective sat back in his chair looking thoughtful. "Yes, I guess we could do that, call it a routine investigation. This is the second time this has happened?"

Cathy nodded. Then she recited the first writing from memory. The detective scrawled it down on a note pad making her repeat each line slowly. Then he asked if she knew the recent one as well. Again she repeated it to him. Once he had finished writing he told her.

"We'll get an expert to look at it this time. Maybe someone in the building will be a match, but don't count on it. More than likely not."

Cathy shrugged her shoulders.

Next he asked her to describe the cat like person in detail as much as she could remember.

Again she did so. It was so ingrained in her mind now, she saw it in her sleep.

The detective again asked her. "You are the only one who sees this person?"

"Apparently." Cathy retorted.

"Hmm." The man shifted in his chair as if thinking. Then he asked, "What about business associates, Miss Lein? Do you have any clients who seem to rub you the wrong way?"

Cathy smiled faintly and replied. "Dr. Paul Davis, the dentist. We just seem to be at odds all the time, but I don't think..."

The detective cleared his throat. Then he asked, "Anyone else?"

"Not that I can think of." Cathy answered truthfully. Then she added, "Oh, wait. Well, Luke's office assistant, Lucy Becker. We don't get along great if you know what I mean."

The detective nodded. He tapped the pad with his pen. "Good point. Anyone else?"

Cathy shook her head.

"Well, if you think of anyone or anything..."

Cathy interrupted. "I know, write it down."

"Thanks for coming by. All right, I guess that is it for now, Miss Lein. Please be as observant as possible, and, be careful "

15. Picturesque

When Cathy got back home she sat down to study her list. Lucy had been with Luke and Jess when the writing on the wall had been discovered the first time. She was at the Bible study all the time and she had come with Luke. Cathy doubted she could have written it. She seemed to be as surprised by it as everyone else. Cathy wriggled in her chair. Then she thought, what about Dr. Paul Davis? He had told her he had seen her at the play. Was this significant? Had she written it down? She turned back pages to look. No, she had forgotten. She added it. Cathy sighed and looked around her living room. She thought to herself, next he'll be asking me if I had any enemies from college or high school. There weren't any that she knew of. What a strange situation to be in.

She and Luke were discussing the police investigation a few days later after supper in her apartment. She was explaining the procedure.

"The police detective said that the handwriting expert said the person who wrote the verses on the laundry room wall was probably left handed from the slant of the lettering. The detective said they examined the writing in the tenants' registry but found no matches. Luke, I am left handed."

He nodded. "Yes, I know, Darlin', but you are not the culprit I am sure."

She said. "Hardly. Now where does that leave us?"

"Don't know, but we'll keep our eyes open for black cats and anything else suspicious."

Cathy gave him a kiss which he returned. Then she spoke. "There is something else, Honey."

"What is it?"

Tina wants us to double date with her and Jim sometime."

His eyebrows raised slightly. "Oh? And how do you feel about that?"

Cathy shook her head. "I don't know. I can't think of a good excuse why not to do it. I told Tina I'd ask you about it."

"Well, maybe we can just think on it for awhile."

Cathy laughed. "Now you sound like John Helper. That sounds good though."

As winter melted into spring, doors seemed to stick more, floorboards began to creek more and little things that would normally be little things began to bother Cathy more. Again she found that there was air in the pipes and she had to call the building supervisor. This time, however, she insisted that he come when Luke was there. Luke came over for lunch so that she could have Max fix her problem again. They ate while he worked. When he had finished she thanked him and he left. He had assured her that she could call him any time if she had problems.

She locked her door after him then went back to the kitchen. "I'm so glad you stayed, Luke. Thank you for being here. I don't want to take any chances."

He nodded then told her. "Any reason to spend time with you is worth it. Come here."

Luke reached out his arms and she came for a secure hug of safety and affection. After a few moments he spoke again. "As much as I hate to leave you, my beauty, I should get back to the office. I have more patients this afternoon. I'll be back soon." He kissed her again.

"See you later, Love. I'll walk with you to the door." Cathy smiled up into his face.

Once she had locked the door behind him she turned and then heard a noise in the hall. Quickly she unlocked the door to see Luke lying face down on the floor. She went to help him and aided him to walk back into her apartment to sit down. She then went to close and lock the door. Turning back she saw him rubbing his ankle.

"Here, I'll take your shoe off." She offered. She got a foot stool and set his leg up on it then removed his shoe and sock. His ankle was slightly puffy on one side.

"Oh no. I guess I sprained it a little."

"Luke, what happened?"

He sighed. "I tripped on a loose floorboard I guess."

She stood up. "Let's get some ice on that." She went to the kitchen to get an ice pack. When she came back she set it under the side of his foot. Then she told him. "Let that sit awhile so it doesn't swell. I'll get the phone so you can call the office."

He told his receptionist, "I should be back in about an hour. Yes I know there are patients already waiting. No emergencies? Good. Well, I just sprained my ankle a little and need some time to take care of it. No, I am all right. Lucy doesn't have to come. I should be able to walk on it in a little bit. Let the patients know

I'll be there or they can reschedule if they want to. Okay. Goodbye."

Cathy protested. "Luke, why didn't you just take the rest of the day off?"

He shook his head. "It will be all right. Just let me rest a little while."

She took the phone back then came to sit near him. "You can stay as long as you need to. Do you want anything?"

"Just you." His eyes were full of love. After a few moments he asked her, "Don't you think you should call Max about the floorboards in the hall?"

"Oh." She got up to make the call.

A short time later, after the hammering had stopped, the door bell rang.

Cathy went to answer it. Max told her that he had hammered down the loose boards outside her door. She thanked him and closed the door again and locked it. In spite of her protests and pleading, Luke did go back to work for a couple of hours. Some patients had rescheduled but a few had waited for him to return. While he was gone Cathy noted the incident in her journal.

One warm Sunday afternoon Cathy and Luke were spending the day in between church services at the Helpers'. John had made prior plans with Luke unknown to Cathy. Luke took her hand and asked, "Come on, Cathy, want to go for a walk with me?"

Cathy looked at Elsie who nodded. "Go ahead dear."

"I guess so, but let me take my sweater in case I need it."

Once outside Luke amended. "Actually we have to ride first before we can go for that walk. It will save time so we won't be late for service tonight."

Cathy turned questioning eyes up to him as John brought the truck up to where they were standing. He reached over to open the passenger door and said, "Come on, climb in."

"I don't know." Cathy sounded fearful.

Luke coaxed her. "Now, Sweetheart, you can trust us. We would never put you in danger. There is a section of land I want to show you and it is too far to walk out there both ways. We wouldn't have enough time. It's all right, believe me." His expression was so tender.

John added. "Miss Cathy, we are beholden to God himself so we could not put you in harms way, one of His own. It is our responsibility to watch out for each other. We're just goin' to ride awhile. Then I will drop you and Luke off to enjoy the countryside. That's all."

She glanced up at Luke's face again and finally stepped up onto the running board with one foot. She took John's out stretched hand as he helped her up the rest of the way. Luke stepped up easily to sit on the outside and he closed the door with a thump.

Once they had reached their destination, several acres at one edge of John and Elsie's property, Cathy was surprised to find John's son Jack waiting there. There were two horses ties to trees beside a small pond where they could eat grass and drink at their leisure.

"Hello, Jack." Cathy greeted him.

Jack and Luke exchanged smiles and Jack waved his hand in greeting. "All set, Dad." Jack told his father.

"Okay then, come on, let's go." John replied. "See you two later."

Jack opened the passenger door to climb into the truck with John and then they drove back the way John had just come.

Cathy exclaimed. "Luke! How are we going to get back?"

Luke smiled and pointed to the two horses who were grazing peacefully a little way from them.

Cathy shook her head. "I have never...ridden...a horse." She stammered.

"Don't worry, Cat. These two are very gentle. They will be tied together and the going will be slow. That is unless you want to go faster. Besides, these are older mares. They won't be in any hurry. It will be fun."

"That's easy for you to say. You know how to ride. Lucas Hoffman, what are you up to?"

Luke stepped close to her and placed a light kiss on her forehead. "Trust me, Darlin'. It will be safe. Come, let's walk a little. I want to show you the pond and the field and the woods." He took her hand and they began to walk. "I love it here. It is so peaceful and serene. I could spend hours, days even, just settin' by the lake or under a shade tree. Can you see the birds?" He pointed.

Cathy shook her head. "No, but I can hear them. It is nice out here." They had gone around the pond and were looking back toward the woods beyond it across from where they were standing now. "Oh, what a beautiful view." Cathy admired her surroundings at last.

He pointed to the pond. "Watch." He said. Luke picked up a rock near the edge of the water and slung it out across the surface. It skimmed and skipped along on top of the water, then finally disappeared beneath the surface. Ripples flowed out smoothly in a circular pattern. "Skippin' rocks." He told her with a smile.

Cathy stepped closer to the water's edge and sat down on the bank. She peered into her reflection on the surface. The water was so clear that she could see small fish swimming underneath and the wrinkles in the sandy bottom of the pond. She looked up.

Luke was taking a picture of the horses by the water. He knew Cathy didn't like having her picture taken so he ventured to ask her first. "Cathy, please let me take a picture of you out here."

She began to protest. "Oh, Luke, I'm not dressed for that. I'm wearing blue jeans and a sweat shirt with a sweater on top of that. My hair's a mess."

"Sweet Cathy, you would look beautiful in a hurricane. Please, Darlin', you look just like a home grown country girl right now—my country girl."

His simplistic manner brought laughter from her. "Well, since you put it so eloquently, how can I refuse? Go ahead."

He led her to where he wanted her to stand and she indulged him. He repeated one of her favorite Proverbs. It was Proverbs 17:22. "'A joyful heart is good medicine,'". Then she heard the click of the camera several times. A gentle breeze had lifted her hair slightly as he snapped his treasured memories.

They walked out into the grassy field under the warmth of the early spring sunshine. Cathy breathed in the sweet aroma of the grass. The gentle breeze washed over them like a renewing spirit. They continued strolling around the pond until they came back to the wooded side where the horses were standing peacefully.

"It is wonderful out here, Luke. It smells so...fresh."

Luke nodded and smiled broadly. Then he pleaded. "Cathy, my sweet, let me take another picture of you by the horses? Please?"

This time she smiled and retorted. "There's a condition."

Luke wrinkled his brow and asked, "What might that be? A kiss perhaps?"

She shook her head and said, "Let me also take your picture. I want to capture that look you have been giving me ever since we got out of the truck." She came closer to embrace him and lean upward for the kiss. It was heart stopping, breath taking, absolutely unforgettable. They kissed again and held each other for a long moment that could have been a lifetime. Over her shoulder Luke could see that the sun was getting lower in the sky. Finally he told her.

"Let's take those pictures, then we will have to start back."

He placed her between the two horses while he reassured her that it would be all right. Again he recited one of their favorite Proverbs as he took a couple of pictures. He quoted from Proverbs 15:30. "'Bright eyes gladden the heart;'". Before she moved away to snap the image she kissed him again, warmly, soundly. She too took several snap shots which finished the film. When she came back to him she expressed her heart.

"Oh, Luke, that captivating look you give me is haunting my dreams."

He embraced and cuddled her. The strength of his emotions almost took his breath away. Finally he forced himself to let her go so that he could instruct and help her up into the saddle. He put the camera in his saddlebag and mounted the lead horse. He had told her to let her body feel the horse's movement and try to match it's stride in order to ride with it, not against it. After a few minutes of slow easy walking she began to feel it's rhythm and commented to him. As they progressed along the path through the woods Luke picked up the pace to a trot. Cathy did not protest. This was a big step toward trust in him on her part he felt. They returned to the farm house just as the family was sitting down to supper.

When they returned to the city to Cathy's apartment building Max hailed them from the office with a cheery greeting. The hour was late as they had stopped and waited for the film to be developed on their way back.

"Let's stop in?" Cathy asked and Luke nodded. She told him of the beautiful day they had had at the farm and showed him the pictures they had taken.

Max remarked. "Oh, these are absolutely beautiful. I see you have duplicates. Please, may I have one of Cathy? It would mean a lot to me. She reminds me of someone I once knew and she is so beautiful here."

"I guess it will be all right." Cathy allowed. "Thank you."

Max took the image as if it were a delicate object. "Thank you, ma'am, sincerely. Thank you."

She nodded and they continued on their way up stairs.

When Luke came back down stairs to get into his car, he automatically checked around the outside as was his occasional habit. He happened to look down as he reached for the driver's door handle. Then he noticed that the rear driver's side tire of his car had been slashed.

16. Double Trouble

Once Cathy had gotten ready for bed she felt a stuffiness in her room. She got back out of bed and went to the window. It should be alright to open it for a few minutes of fresh, cool air. The window appeared to be stuck. Cathy pulled the shade up out of her way and pushed the curtains aside as she struggled with the window. Finally she succeeded in pulling it up. The curtains billowed as cool air surrounded her. Suddenly there were several flashes of light in her eyes. Quickly she forced the stubborn window to close and pulled the shade down. The curtains settled back against the shade in silence. Cathy blinked several times trying to clear her vision of the spots. What had happened? Thinking of her day and the pictures they had taken, the flashing reminded her of a camera's flash bulb. There had been no sound that she could hear.

"Oh no." She breathed. She reached for her bedroom phone to call the police.

"No, I didn't see anything." She responded to the officer's question. "How could I with that light flashing in my face?"

"Oh, fine, so there is nothing you can do. Yes, I understand. Whoever it was would be gone by the time someone arrived if it was a prowler. Well, thank you. Good bye. What? Yes, I am working with a detective, but I can't recall his name right at the moment. I will call back tomorrow and ask for him. I do have his card, just not right in front of me. Yes, I know, write it down. Thank you for your help."

She hung up the phone. She started to dial Luke's number then stopped. No need to wake him. It was late enough already. Cathy sighed and glanced at her lone window in the room. The shade was drawn and curtains too. She got back into bed and settled for a restless night.

It was exactly eight o'clock when her phone shrilled in the morning. Startled, she bolted up right in bed and picked it up. "Hello." After a pause she remembered the rest of her greeting.

"This is Dr. Davis. I have another emergency surgery this morning. Are you going to be available today?"

"Oh yes, of course. I will be right here, Dr. Davis."

"Just checking. Good bye."

The abrupt click seemed unusually loud to her this day. Then she realized that her head was pounding in a head ache. Cathy sighed and laid back down. She needed more sleep. Surely the phone would wake her. Besides, the machine was there after all.

The next time she heard the phone it was about 12:25 in the afternoon.

This time she stated. "Lein's Answering Line."

"Cathy, it's Luke. I'm taking a very short lunch at my desk so I thought I'd call. How are you doing today, Love?"

"Oh, I'm still in bed. Dr. Davis woke me promptly at eight o'clock and I had such a head ache I just laid back down again. Oh, Luke, something really weird happened last night after you left. I didn't want to call and wake you since it was so late anyway."

"Oh no. Are you all right?"

"Yes."

"You sure?"

"Yes, yes. I'll tell you about it later. You must be tired too."

"Yeah, I sure am. I have something to tell you, also." He told her about the tire incident. She insisted on reporting it, but he said since it had been dark he doubted anyone had seen it happen and there was nothing to go on.

"Well, I'll write it down for sure." She concluded. Next Cathy asked him. "What time did you get to bed after that tire got fixed?"

"I don't know, but sleeping fast didn't do the trick. It's been hectic here today. Well, I will be over after closing. If I am late it's due to patient catch up, you know."

"Okay. I understand, Love. See you tonight."

Cathy got up and stretched. At least her head wasn't pounding any more. She automatically checked the answering machine for any messages she might have missed. Thankfully there were none. She went to the bathroom for a quick shower. The rest of the day passed with little interruption. Dr. Davis did not have to call back. She was glad that Tina had to work this Monday. She certainly would not have felt up to morning Bible study today. But she didn't want to refuse their time together either. She liked Tina and enjoyed their morning talks. Thank you, Lord, she sighed. The afternoon passed quickly. She had time to note the latest strange incidents in her journal.

When Cathy saw Luke that evening, she remarked that he looked as though he hadn't gotten much sleep either. Then she confided to him. "These things are becoming ridiculous, Luke. Now you could be in danger because of me."

Luke came to put his arms around her. "Now, now, don't get carried away about it. Let's just take one thing at a time. Don't worry about me. You are the important one it seems in all this. You are the one being stalked. It seems so hard to believe this is real. Oh, Cat, I pray for your safety always. I wish this could be solved and over with." His embrace tightened.

She was nodding and then pressed her cheek to his chest. Softly she told him. "You are my strength, Love."

The next Bible study group meeting would be at Luke's apartment. Cathy had mixed feelings about that. She hadn't been to a man's place. Granted, there would be plenty of people there. It wasn't as if she and Luke weren't acquainted with each other. She did trust him. It was just that it was her first time there she had told herself. Cathy and Penny had developed a pleasing working relationship. Cathy took all calls on Wednesday evenings so that Penny could attend church. Penny took Thursday evenings to allow Cathy to attend the group studies. Luke would take her and Jess out to supper before hand. Then they would go to his place.

"I can't wait to see your place, Luke." Jess remarked. Then she asked, "Will Elsie be there?"

"Oh yes." Luke replied. "Everyone who usually comes to the studies will be there. Lucy is also coming this time." They had left the restaurant and Luke was driving through the city. He glanced at his lady who sat beside him in the front seat. "Cathy, how are you feeling?"

"Nervous. But that is just me. I can't help it."

"It will be okay, Cat." Jess assured her. "It is going to be fun."

Cathy nodded. "I know. I really enjoyed the meal, Luke. The food was excellent."

He nodded. "I like that particular Chinese restaurant. I'm glad you did too. Jess?"

"Yes. I like Chinese too. How long will it take to get to your place, Luke?"

"Not long, Jess. We need to be there before the others start arriving."

Cathy asked, "Is Lucy coming by herself?"

"I don't know. She didn't say, but she was in a hurry to leave the office."

As always John and Elsie had brought extra chairs. To Jess's delight their daughter Ella came with them. Jack was usually left in charge of the family in both parents absence. Jack was a senior in high school and was planning for college in the upcoming fall. Lucy and Tina arrived by themselves. Cathy noticed that Lucy was dressed as if she were going dancing at an exclusive club. Her dress was silky and shimmery. The back was bare and the dress was sleeveless. Her hair had been fashioned in a pug style revealing her glittering ear rings and necklace against her bare skin. Cathy felt her skin crawl as she assumed Lucy was still trying to impress Luke. She tried to ignore the feeling but her emotions would not let her dismiss it. Cathy felt plain as usual, but she tried to avoid dwelling on the comparison. She told herself that it was Luke who had told her that physical beauty was superficial. What had he said about the spirit? She went to whisper to Elsie, but, just then, John called for everyone's attention.

"First off," John began, "we want to thank Luke for invitin' us all here."

Applause erupted.

Luke was shaking his head. "Now you folks know I am happy to be a part of such a wonderful endeavor. Besides, it is Jesus who is the focus of our attention, not me. Oh, and before I forget, we have Elsie, Cathy and Tina to thank for refreshments afterward." He glanced over at his friend and mentor. "Go ahead, John." Luke sat down beside Cathy. She noticed he was wearing his smooth silk shirt that she had seen him in on their first date. He also wore a tie this evening. She admired her handsome man and silently thanked God for him.

John was speaking. "Tonight, I thought we would concentrate on friendship since we have such a fine group here. So, let's start with a familiar verse. I'll recite it and I want someone to tell me the address, the book, chapter and verse. Okay, here goes. 'A friend loves at all times,'. Now, who has the address? I'll tell ya it is in the book of..."

Tina interrupted, "Proverbs, the book of Proverbs."

John nodded. "That's right, Tina. Can you give us the rest of the address?"

Tina shook her head as color began to creep into her cheeks.

John assured her. "That's okay, Tina. Any one else?"

"I know where it is." Luke stated.

"Me too." Elsie agreed.

"Well, let's give some of the newer people a try." John suggested. Following a short pause of silence he allowed. "All right, here's the rest of the verse. 'And a brother is born for adversity.'" John looked around the room then encouraged, "Okay, come on, someone, guess."

Cathy queried. "Chapter 17?"

John smiled. "Very good, Cathy. Do you know which verse?"

Cathy shook her head. Then she told him. "No, but I like the Proverbs."

"Come on, we are so close to the right answer." John continued. "We have Proverbs 17. This is an easy one to figure out. That is a clue."

Lucy guessed. "Ha, verse 17."

"All right, Lucy got it." John chuckled. "Well, that one took three people to get to where we're goin'. Here's another one. This time I have to give you all of it because the part we want is in the second half of the verse. It's also in Proverbs. Here 'tis. 'A man of too many friends comes to ruin. But there is a friend who sticks closer than a brother.' Okay, now where is this one?"

A soft voice spoke up. "I've got it. It's chapter 18 verse 24."

John exclaimed, "Yes, very well done, Ruth. Now the next one will be in a different book. If you know who this friend is, you'll be able to figure out this next one. Ready? Here goes. '"You are My friends if you do what I command you. No longer do I call you slaves, for the slave does not know what his master is doing; but I have called you friends, for all things that I have heard from My Father I have made known to you."'

Jess raised her hand. "Oh, I know who is speaking."

John prompted her. "Go ahead, Jess."

"That's Jesus."

"That's right, Jess. Very nice. Now can someone else provide the reference?" John asked. He wanted to praise Jess who was right on track but he didn't want to ask her anything too difficult.   John knew his daughter's capabilities and guessed Jess'es to be similar. He admired their simple honesty and sincerity. Elsie had helped him to accept his daughter's condition. She had been a pillar of patience and understanding in trying to get across to him his daughter's simple mind.

Someone else spoke finally. "I think it is one of the Gospels, but I don't know which one."

John nodded. "Okay, here's a clue. Who is speakin' right now?"

Luke laughed then said, "It's from the book of John, right?"

John smiled his agreement. Then he encouraged his friend. "Well, what's the rest of it, Luke?"

"I think it's John 15:14–15."

John replied simply. "Can't fool you, my friend."

Then John launched into a ten or fifteen minute sermon on friendship with lots of examples of Biblical figures for support. Everyone was captivated by his unique expressiveness. Finally he announced time for singing which would be followed by refreshments. He closed with a prayer of thanksgiving following the singing.

Cathy came up to him during refreshments and commented. "John, you are wonderful. You make Bible study so much fun."

Jess nodded her agreement as did Ella.

Then Ella said, "Daddy is cool."

Everyone who heard laughed and added their love to that.

"Luke, this is truly wonderful. I wouldn't miss a meeting for anything now." Cathy told him.

He placed a light kiss on her forehead. "I am so glad you feel that way, Love."

She nodded and smiled.

"Hi, Luke."

They both looked up to see Lucy standing near him.

"Hi, Lucy." He replied easily. "Are you enjoying yourself?"

She shrugged her shoulders and leaned down to whisper into his ear. Cathy wished she could hear it but she did not.

Luke replied. "Sorry, Lucy. That's not going to happen."

Lucy made a disgusting noise and walked away.

"Luke?" Cathy seized her opportunity.

Luke shook his head. "Nothing important at all, Darlin'."

Cathy persisted. "But, surely you've noticed Lucy's...dress."

Luke waved a hand. "I told you before, Honey. Outward beauty is superficial. It's what's inside that counts."

Cathy laughed and he smiled at her. "That's better." He said. Following a short silence he asked, "Cathy, have you given any more thought to the idea of double dating with Tina and Jim?"

Cathy shook her head then replied. "Actually no, but right now you could probably almost convince me to double date with Lucy, but you would have to be my date."

It was Luke's turn to laugh. "So, do you want to do it?"

"I suppose so. You want to talk to Tina now?"

He nodded. They went to discuss it with the other woman.

The four of them went out together on a Friday evening. Both Cathy and Tina had the week end off so Tina would work on Monday. They had decided to eat at a popular restaurant then attend a musical concert. Tina had styled Cathy's hair piling it in an updo on top of her head. Both women had dressed up for the occasion and received corsages from their dates. Luke had offered to drive so they could all go in the same vehicle. Jim left his car at the girls apartment building. Since Max was in the office when they were leaving, Luke asked if he would mind taking a couple of pictures of the couples. He agreed to provided that he could have one of them once they were developed. Of course that was agreeable. Cathy wondered why he wanted another picture. But she dismissed the thought thinking he was just being polite to accommodate them.

They were eating at a steak house, their first destination. Cathy sat next to Luke and across from Jim.

Tina chided Jim teasingly. "Now, please, Jim, no cat jokes tonight."

"Really." Her date stated.Then he looked at Cathy and asked, "So, how have you been, Cat?"

"All right." Cathy replied. Then, after a thought, she added, "I have my guardian angel here." She touched Luke's arm as she smiled.

Tina smiled. "I'd like one of those. How do you get a guardian angel?"

"Pray." Luke told her. "The Bible tells us in Psalms 91:11, 'For He will give His angels charge concerning you,to guard you in all your ways.'"

Tina set down her drink and commented. "Wow, that is neat. I like that."

Jim cleared his throat then spoke. "Okay, enough Bible stuff. Let's talk about something else."

Cathy looked at Luke, then at Jim. Finally she spoke. "Well then, what would you like to talk about, Jim? How about the costume party at the Helpers' farm?"

Tina responded. "Oh, yes, wasn't that great fun?"

Luke nodded as he swallowed his bite of food. Then he commented. "I especially enjoyed seeing all the pretty ladies in their costume gowns."

Tina waved her sweet roll with a sweeping gesture then said, "That was really cool the way those guys swooped down to make an entrance, Superman and Peter Pan and the way you and John rode in on your horses, Luke. I will always remember that day." She bit into her roll and made a pleasing sound. "Delicious." She said with emphasis when she had finished it.

Jim agreed. "Yeah, that was pretty slick. How'd you decide to be the Lone Ranger, Luke?"

Luke swallowed his food and then replied. "Actually, it was Cathy's idea. She was trying to associate me with animals and came up with it. I liked it and so John chose to be my side kick."

Cathy looked up and asked, "So, Jim, what made you pick a cat costume?"

Luke picked up his drink.

"Oh, c'mon, Cat. Do you really have to ask? I told you. I wanted to surprise you, Cat. Don't you get it?"

She was nodding. "Okay. Well then, where did you get the costume?"

Tina spoke. "I showed him that great costume shop in the mall. They have a terrific selection. I'll bet you two went to the same place. Right?"

Luke and Cathy nodded.

Cathy was nibbling at her steak, cutting it into small pieces. She spoke after swallowing a bit. "Still, that was one of the best experiences I've had. I will always remember it, among many others at the Helpers'." She gazed at Luke who was sitting beside her.

Her expressive smile was so sincere, her eyes so bright, he wanted to capture that serene look and keep it forever. Impulsively he reached into his suit jacket pocket and brought out his camera. He quickly looked into the view finder and snapped his portrait.

"Luke! What on earth are you doing?" Cathy exclaimed.

"I know I didn't ask, Honey. I just had to capture that lovely face." Then he turned. "Tina and Jim, sit closer so I can..."

Jim took his cue and put his arm around his date leaning close to her. Both smiled as Luke took another picture. Then Jim motioned for Luke to pass him the camera. Luke then put his arm around Cathy and they too were captured together. Then Luke put the camera back into his pocket. After a few minutes of silence while they ate he commented. "It's nice to have happy memories to share."

"This is truly wonderful." Cathy agreed. "I am looking forward to the concert too. It should be great. This food is absolutely great."

Tina also expressed her joy. "I am having a wonderful time. I will always treasure this too. I am glad we doubled. Aren't you, Jim?"

"Sure."

Then Tina spoke again. "Luke, we will all get copies of the pictures?"

"Oh naturally. There will be more. You can count on it. I brought an extra roll of film just in case we need it. May I say, you two ladies are very beautiful."

Both of the women smiled sweetly.

When they had finished dessert Luke drove them to the concert. Jim and Tina rode in close comfort in the back seat.

Following the concert, Jim and Tina had exited a little way ahead of Luke and Cathy. The younger couple laughed and talked as they walked briskly along the tar. Other people were doing the same, but the lot was not crowded as not everyone had come out of the building yet. Luke and Cathy strolled leisurely enjoying each others company. Jim and Tina reached the car first.

"Did you enjoy it, Babe?" Jim asked.

Tina nodded and reached up to hug his neck. Suddenly she made a noise of surprised exclamation as she was dipped backward and Jim kissed her soundly.

As they continued walking through the parking lot, Luke and Cathy heard screeching sounds approaching from behind them. Out of the corner of his eye Luke saw a car weaving through the lot toward them. He quickly pulled Cathy to him as it sped past, barely missing her, wavering uncertainly as it traveled out of the parking lot and away.

17. It's About Truth

"Cathy, are you all right?" Luke's voice was anxious.

Cathy saw Luke's face pale. He was still holding her. She nodded and turned her head to stare at the now empty space in front of them. Both turned as they heard foot steps. Tina and Jim had come running up to them.

Finally Luke spoke. "Jim, did you see that? Did you get the license plate number?"

Jim shook his head. "No, sorry, man. It went by so fast we didn't realize what had happened right away. Is she okay?"

"Yes." Luke said. "I didn't get it either. It came so close I barely had time to pull her out of the way." He still looked around them. None of the other people seemed to be aware of what had just almost taken place. People were walking past without seeing anything out of the ordinary.

Tina put a hand on Cathy's arm. "Cathy? Are you sure you are all right?"

"Yes, thank you." Cathy managed to speak.

Luke told them, "At least I can identify the model and color of the car I'm pretty sure. Too bad I couldn't get a picture, but I was more concerned about Cathy's safety. Come on, let's get going before anything else crazy happens." He walked with Cathy to his car, holding her around her waist. Then he opened the passenger side door for her and waited to close it after she had sat down. Jim and Tina got into the back seat. Luke checked as he walked around to the driver's side. Then he went to the front and opened the hood. Everything looked normal so he closed it again.

Once Luke had gotten into the car Jim asked, "Is everything all right, man?"

Luke nodded. "Just makin' sure." He started the engine. It ran smoothly. Upon parting company with Tina and Jim at the apartment building, Luke told Cathy he was going to the police station to report the incident. He asked if she wanted to go with him, but she shook her head and said she would write it down. She felt there was no point in her talking to someone else when she would have to repeat it to the detective she was working with anyway. Luke walked her up stairs to her own apartment, seeing her safely inside before he had kissed her and left.

It wasn't until the following week that she heard back from the police detective. He wanted Cathy to come to the station to see if she could identify a suspect in a line up. He had explained that the investigation of those who attended the concert and had driven a vehicle matching Luke's description had been questioned and they needed corroboration from her. She had insisted that Luke accompany her this time. She was not going to do this alone. She didn't think she would be able to identify anyone. Fear and dread welled up inside of her even though the detective had promised that she would not be seen by any of the suspects.

Luke came around as she stepped out and closed the car

door. He took her hand and placed a kiss on her forehead. "Just be honest, Honey. That's all you can do. You are so good at doing that. I love you. Remember, Jesus and I are with you."

Cathy released his hand to put both arms around him for a secure hug which he returned. She looked up with wide, tear glazed eyes. "You are so special, Luke. I don't know what I would do without you." She pressed her cheek to his chest then pulled away to wipe her eyes. As they began to walk slowly he took her hand again and held it the whole time they were in the station.

As she had suspected, Cathy did not recognize any of the suspects. The detective she had been working with introduced himself to Luke afterward. He had explained to them that one of the men in the line up had been brought in on a charge of driving while intoxicated, D.W.I. on the evening of the concert. Furthermore, he had been driving the vehicle that closely matched Luke's description. The suspect claimed to have no knowledge of the incidents relating to Cathy's stalker. The suspect did not know how to write poetry and had never owned or rented a cat costume. He didn't know anyone named Cathy or Cat.

Once back in Luke's car Cathy said. "I knew I wouldn't be of any help to him."

Luke observed. "This looks like an isolated incident and not related to our troubles."

"Our troubles?" She repeated.

Luke nodded. "Anything that affects you affects me and vice versa, Love. Would you like to go and get something to eat?"

She shook her head. "No. I'm not hungry. Besides, don't you have to get back to your patients? You took the morning off for me."

"Yes, but not until I am sure you are all right. I'll take you home then."

She nodded. She knew it had been difficult for Luke to rearrange patient scheduling again on her behalf. She felt responsible for his accident outside her apartment when he had sprained his ankle. Maybe that had been meant for her. She did not reveal these thoughts to him however. She rode in sullen silence as he drove.

Once back inside her apartment he did not leave her right away. She asked if he wanted something to eat. He had told her only if she was going to have something. She shook her head. He led her to sit together on the couch.

Taking her hands he said, "Cathy, do you know when I was first attracted to you?"

She looked up with a surprised expression. She was not expecting this query. She shrugged her shoulders but said nothing.

He continued. "Remember, the first time you came into my office? You were pitching your new answering service business. You wore a dark blue business suit and had your hair pulled back in a pony tail. With those glasses on you reminded me of Dianna Prince. Then, of course, I pictured you in a Wonder Woman costume."

This brought a slight chuckle from her.

Luke's voice became soft and tender. "You know, I just couldn't get you out of my mind ever since then. I admired your guts, but there was a gentle spirit behind that outward determination. I think God let me see you through His eyes. That's why I asked you out on that first date. I just had to get to know you better." He started to lean toward her.

Cathy reached up to hug his neck as they kissed.

Finally she pulled back and stood. Her voice was almost a whisper when she spoke. "Luke, if we don't stop this I will be leading you into the bedroom."

He also stood. "Time to go back to the office. See you later, my sweet love." He walked toward the door. Turning back he said, "Now don't forget to lock it." Then he went out. He waited in the hallway until he heard the click of the lock, then he left. He had certainly succeeded in changing her mood.

Cathy busied herself doing house cleaning. She didn't want to face the truth of her adult feelings for Luke. She didn't understand how he could tell her such a beautiful thing. He had said, "God let me see you through His eyes." Cathy wished she could understand this. How could she have become so intimately acquainted with such a loving and honest man? Why had God given her such a wonderful experience? Was God's love that deep? She recalled a verse in Psalms. "I will give thanks to You, for I am fearfully and wonderfully made;" Cathy stopped what she was doing to get her Bible from her bedroom. She searched and found the reference. It was Psalms 139:14. The rest of the verse read: "Wonderful are Your works, And my soul knows it very well." She read the entire chapter. Then she read through the rest of the book to the end of Psalm 150. She felt awed by God's goodness to her.

The next time she saw Luke she expressed her feelings about God to him. She also said that Luke was fearfully and wonderfully made. He had replied that Psalm 139 was an uplifting one. John had called while they were together and told them that the next Bible meeting would be on truth. He had said to brush up on the book of Romans and to find some other related passages to be ready to share.

Once Cathy had explained the phone call she then told him. "Okay, I am going to cheat." She went to her bedroom to get her study Bible. She put it down on the coffee table and sat beside Luke. "I have my good teacher here," Cathy said, "so we can do our study together and I'll be good and ready for the lesson on Thursday."

"But, I don't have my study Bible with me," Luke protested teasingly, "just my little pocket Bible."

"Well, we'll just have to share mine." Cathy replied. She opened it to the book of Romans.

The following day Cathy was busy catching up on her bookkeeping. It was early evening when she decided to take her garbage out. She was on her way down stairs when she over heard Tina and Jim apparently arguing.

Tina was saying, "You could have said something to me about it."

Jim retorted. "Yeah, and how would you have reacted, Babe? Just like you are doing now."

Tina sighed. "It's about truth, Jim. Do you know anything about that?"

"Well, we weren't committed. There wasn't anything serious."

"You've got that right, Jim. No, nothing serious. Good bye, Jim."

Cathy heard Tina almost running up stairs then her apartment door slammed shut. Tina hadn't seen Cathy because Cathy still had to turn the corner to go down the next flight of stairs. When she got outside she saw Jim's car pulling out of the parking space to leave. Cathy deposited her garbage bags and turned to go back inside. Cathy felt for her friend. She wondered if she should knock on her door. Luke would be coming soon. Cathy decided to go back up stairs and write a note in case Luke came and she wasn't there. She pinned it to the outside of her door and went back down stairs to the next floor. She knocked at Tina's door.

"Go away." Tina called.

"Tina, it's Cathy."

Tina came and opened her door to let her friend inside.

Cathy explained. "Tina, I was taking my garbage down and I accidentally over heard you and Jim arguing. I'm sorry, but I wanted to see you."

Tina responded with a tearful embrace. Once she had calmed enough to speak she told Cathy why they had argued. "I found out through someone else that Jim is dating Lucy Becker."

Cathy's mouth opened in surprise.

Tina nodded. "I've only seen her a couple of times, at Bible studies come to think of it, but I am no competition for that."

"Welcome to the club." Cathy mused. "But, Luke says he is not interested in her that way and I believe him. He says your inner beauty, your spiritual beauty, is what really counts. You know, like in Proverbs 31. I'm not that but you know what I mean."

Tina nodded. "It hurt to find that out. I thought we had a good thing going together. We like to do a lot of the same things and he is funny and easy to be with. It didn't bother him it seems, but I don't want to be competition or be compared to someone else. I want a serious relationship like you and Luke have. Is that asking too much from a guy?"

Cathy shook her head. "No, my friend, you just have to find

the right guy. Maybe God has someone better in mind for you." Cathy surprised herself at her perceptive statement. Then she said, "Tina, I have to get back. Luke should be here by now. Do you want to come up stairs with me for awhile?"

Tina was shaking her head. "No, thanks though. I will be all right. Thanks for caring. You are a good friend, Cathy."

Cathy embraced her friend again and then turned to go. Before leaving she told Tina, "Call me if you need to. Promise?"

Tina nodded and Cathy went out.

The Bible study on truth was held at Cathy's apartment. John began by picking 16 people to each read one chapter of the book of Romans. Once that had been accomplished John asked if anyone had a question or comment before he began.

Cathy stood. "Yes. I want to say that my guardian angel here," she reached over to pat Luke's arm, "is the embodiment of what it says in Romans 12:2 'And do not be conformed to this world, but be transformed by the renewing of your mind, so that you may prove what the will of God is, that which is good and acceptable and perfect.' Luke has been my role model in this. Yes, I know I can't put him up higher than he ought to be. I know the difference between what Jesus has done for me and my love for Luke. God has shown me that. But, God has also given us to each other and it is a wonderful gift." She sat down.

Next, Tina stood. "Well, I guess I have to claim a verse for my situation. It's not exactly in Romans, but it deals with our subject. Is that okay, John?"

John nodded. "Go ahead, Tina."

She continued. "Okay, it's John 8:32 where Jesus says, 'and you will know the truth, and the truth will make you free.' You see, I just dumped my boyfriend for not telling me the truth. He was seeing someone else while going with me and, well, it hurt, so I said good bye and now I'm trying to get back to the Bible more. I believe truth is very important. Thank you." She sat down.

John immediately bowed his head and prayed for God's love and support for Tina. Following his prayer she thanked him. Then he asked if anyone else had another reference to share. When silence prevailed he began to explain that we need to uphold truth. It makes it easier to live in this crazy complex world of ours. He said, "Sometimes the Bible seems to be ideal, out of touch, but it is right on the mark." Then he named the section that he wanted to concentrate on. Finally he concluded with Romans 8:38–39. It tells us, 'For I am convinced that neither death nor life, nor angels nor principalities, nor things present, nor things to come, nor powers, nor height, nor depth, nor any other created thing, shall be able to separate us from the love of God, which is in Christ Jesus our Lord.' Now, if there is nothing else, let's break for refreshments. Thank ya all for comin'.'"

Everyone stood and clapped for John's lecture. Then they proceeded slowly to the kitchen as people began to converse with one another.

Cathy and Luke found a corner in which to sit together.

Cathy remarked. "Wow, John explains things so that it is easy to understand. It makes me wonder why everyone doesn't believe the Bible."

Luke smiled then told her. "I seem to remember someone saying 'You want me to go to a Bible study?'"

Cathy also smiled and nodded. "Okay, you have me there."

As Tina came out of the kitchen a male voice spoke to her.

"Excuse me, Tina, may I sit with you?"

Tina looked over to see a young red headed man wearing glasses who was looking somewhat hesitant. He continued to speak to her.

"My name is Scott Harrington. I've seen you at Thursday studies and I wanted to talk to you, but I wasn't sure, until tonight." He stammered a little. "I mean, I didn't know if you were taken, dating someone, you know. Anyway, may I sit with you? Maybe we could get acquainted?"

Tina nodded.

Luke told Cathy that Tina had captured a man's attention.

Cathy immediately commented. "Oh, that's good."

Luke nodded. "I thought you'd say something like that."

Elsie was sitting with Ella and Jess, but many people went over to speak to Elsie and to John.

Luke mentioned to Cathy that Tina and Scott were leaving together when he saw them going toward the door after they had spoken to John briefly. She nodded and smiled.

Luke asked her, "Why is it that women get so excited about a couple getting together?"

"We like to see people happy, Love."

"Are you happy, Sweetheart?" He asked her.

She nodded. "Right now I am on top of the world."

18. Chase the Cat

"Cathy, did Elsie tell you?"

"Tell me what, Jess?"

Cathy and Jess were sitting in an ice cream shop, the one she and Luke had gone to following the play, on an early Saturday afternoon. Cathy had called the veterinarian's office to let him know that she and Jess were going out. Luke had gone on farm calls that morning and wasn't back yet. Cathy had left a note on her door to remind him.

Jess answered. "About the camp out at their farm."

Cathy looked puzzled. "Camp out?"

Jess nodded as she scooped her spoon into her banana split. "Yes, the camp out on their farm on Memorial Day week end. It will be on Saturday night. It is going to be great fun. It's just their family and the people they invite. It won't be as big as the costume party. I hope they do that again next fall. That was great fun."

Cathy stirred her milk shake with her straw. "I have never been on a camp out. What do you do, Jess?"

Jess shrugged her shoulders then answered. "I don't know either, but Ella says there will be a cook out, fishing, maybe swimming too, I guess. That is, if the weather is warm enough."

Next Cathy asked, "No costumes this time?"

"No, just regular clothes, but you have to bring something warm enough to sleep in."

"Sounds like fun, Jess." Cathy took a bite of her caramel Sundae. Then she said, "I am glad we scheduled this trip. This is nice to get out by ourselves. You are usually so busy you know, Jess."

Jess giggled.

The following Monday morning Tina arrived at Cathy's for their time together. Tina set down her Bible on the coffee table and turned to Cathy.

"Cathy, sit down. I want to tell you about what has happened to me." She was smiling.

They sat on the couch together.

Tina continued. "There's a guy who introduced himself to me at the last group Bible study. His name is Scott Harrington." She named the church he attended.

Cathy now smiled too and nodded.

Tina continued. "Well, anyway, he took me home after the meeting and we talked. It turns out he has a slight speech impediment, which I don't mind. He stammers and stutters a little. It doesn't bother me, but I guess it bothers him. Well, he's kind of shy. He asked me to go to church with him yesterday. We went to both services and spent the whole day together. Jim never wanted to go to church."

Again Cathy nodded.

"Cathy, he is so different from other guys I have dated. He is cute too. Have you seen him at the group studies?"

Cathy replied. "I may have, but I don't recall. You'll just have to introduce me to him."

Tina nodded fervently. "He is an only child. Maybe that's why he is shy. We've lived in the same city but never met. Well, we did go to different high schools. I still can't believe it. He is so easy to talk to and I just go on and on. You know me. But, he doesn't seem to mind." Tina laughed. Then she exclaimed. "Wow."

Cathy took her friend's hands. "See, you never know what God has in store for you. Let's pray and thank Him."

Once Tina had calmed to an easy state of mind the two of them held their small Bible study. They used the book of Ruth this time. When Tina got ready to go, Cathy gave her a warm hug of friendship. As Tina went out Cathy said, "Keep me posted." Tina nodded, still smiling. Then Cathy locked her door.

When Luke arrived that evening she had much to discuss with him. She threw her arms around his neck and smiled up into his face. His kiss was warm and soothing. She sighed and led him to the kitchen. "I have a lot to tell you, Honey."

He responded. "That's nice. You had a good day then?"

She nodded. "Yes. Tina has a new boyfriend, from the group study. His name is Scott Harrington."

Luke nodded.

Cathy asked. "You know him?"

"I know who he is. I don't really know him well. That's nice. She isn't seeing Jim any more?"

Cathy facial expression changed abruptly. She shook her head. "Luke, did you know that Jim was also dating your office assistant Lucy while he was supposedly dating Tina?"

Surprise was evident on the man's face. He shook his head. "She hasn't said anything to me about that. But I don't encourage her to discuss personal matters unless she wants to. In fact, I don't encourage her at all."

"Uh ha." Cathy came to sit on his lap. "How about me?"

His arms came easily around her and his lips came eagerly to hers. After a long moment he spoke softly. "You get lots of encouragement...and love."

Cathy murmured contentedly and rested her cheek against his chest. They sat together in silence for a time, savoring each other's presence. Finally Cathy looked up and spoke. "It still amazes me how safe and relaxed I feel in your arms, my Darling."

His kiss was eager, captivating, dizzying. Cathy slid out of his embrace and stood. She turned and went to the refrigerator. Her senses were still screaming at her. She said something about supper and took a package of hamburger out. Then she turned to him again.

"Luke, where are we going, I mean, with us?"

He looked at her and smiled a little. Then he answered with a quote from Ecclesiastes 3:1. "My Darlin' Cathy, there is a time for everything. 'There is an appointed time for everything. And there is a time for every event under heaven—'. But it is not our time yet. You are not really safe."

She had taken the meat to the counter and was preparing it for cooking. "I don't understand. Nothing has happened for quite a while now."

"Yes, I know, but the stalker hasn't been caught yet. It isn't over I am afraid."

She sighed and nodded as she prepared the meat. Finally she remembered. "Luke, do you know anything about a cook out at the Helpers'?"

"Oh, of course, I did forget. Sure do. Memorial Day week end they have a family outing and camp out in the woods."

"In the woods?"

He nodded. "You sound surprised, Honey. Didn't you know."

"Luke, I've never been to a camp out. Jess didn't say anything about sleeping in the woods."

Luke laughed. Then he said, "You make it sound barbaric."

Cathy started to move to put her hands on her hips but suddenly realized her hands were greasy from the meat and she stopped. "What are you getting me into?"

"Relax, Honey. It will be great fun, just like the costume party. Oh." Luke suddenly realized that the costume party hadn't ended on a happy note. "Don't worry, there shouldn't be any black cat people in the woods, just bear, deer, squirrels and such."

"Bear?"

"Yes, but they rarely go near humans. Don't be afraid. There will be plenty of people around. It's John and Elsie's extended family outing. Bring some warm clothes to sleep in." Luke advised.

"Clothes?" Cathy asked.

He nodded.

"Luke, I want to open the window in the bedroom for awhile to let some outside air in. Would you open it? I'll have you close it after supper. I don't want to do it myself."

He rose to do as she had asked.

When he returned she asked him, "Did you see anything unusual outside?"

"No, nothing."

"Weird things happen to me when I do it. Supper is almost

ready."

She had become accustom to cooking and baking for them. Sometimes she would pretend that they were already married. She thought about what he had recently told her about her situation. Maybe he would propose in the future then. She couldn't see their relationship just going on the way it was without something happening. She still marveled at her adult feelings for this man. She used to shrink away from any serious approaches from the opposite sex. Now she trusted and secretly wanted this man to approach her. She wished more than ever that her situation would come to some kind of resolution. She decided she would pray about it.

By the time they had finished the dish washing and clean up after the meal night had fallen.

Cathy remembered the window. "Luke, will you close the bedroom window now?"

She followed behind him to enter the room. The breeze was soft and cool from the night air. She did not turn on the light as she thought the dull light from the window would be enough. He stepped to the window and began to pull it down over the screen. As he reached up he saw a dark shadow move on the fire escape. Cathy had come to stand beside him. She pointed and put her hand over her mouth. Once he had closed the window she pulled down the shade and drew the curtains. Then she took his hand to silently exit the room.

Once back in the living room she spoke. "Luke, did you see it?"

"I saw something move. It was dark. I couldn't see it clearly."

"It must have been the cat person." Cathy concluded.

"How could you tell?" Luke asked. "Could you see it?"

She shook her head. "I couldn't see it either, but it must have been."

"Call the police?" He asked.

She threw up her hands. "It's gone now. Oh, I'd better write it down. What's the date today?"

He supplied it. Then he said, "Don't let your imagination run away with you. Write exactly what you did see, not what you think it was."

"Yes doctor." She retorted as she wrote in her notebook.

The Helpers' had also invited Tina and Scott to their outing, Luke and Cathy, and a couple of other church families with children. The weather turned out sunny and cooperative with no rain predicted for any of the week end days. Although the sun was warm the air was still cool. It was pleasant with no humidity as yet, with a gentle, soothing breeze. The men busied themselves putting up tents while the women organized the supplies. The children, with Jack and several of the other boys near his age to supervise, were sent to gather wood for the evening fire that would warm them as night approached. They had gone from the farm house in the hay wagon which John had hitched to his truck. They had settled in a clearing within a thickly wooded section of the Helpers' land. By the time camp had been set up lunch out of coolers was after two o'clock.

After lunch the women cleaned up while the men and some of the children went fishing. Elsie explained to Cathy and Tina that this was one week end when the family didn't attend church. They would have their own Bible study and singing time after breakfast on Sunday morning.

Supper consisted of grilled hamburgers and hot dogs on the

barbecue grill while Jack supervised getting the camp fire started. Following supper and clean up, in which everyone participated, there was a sing along, marshmallow toasting and story swapping time. John had brought his guitar for the sing along.

The hour was late once all of the children had been settled into their sleeping bags. Luke and Cathy had stolen a few minutes of solitude. Luke was sitting with his back against a tree with Cathy leaning against him. His arms were around her and she held onto his hands.

She finally commented. "What an amazing day."

"Mm. Tomorrow will be also. We're going to have fish for breakfast."

"Really?"

Then he asked her, "Are you cold?"

"Oh, not now." She smiled up at him.

"You know, we should get to bed too."

She sighed.

They both got up to walk back to the tent area.

"Well, good night, Darlin'" Luke gave her a kiss, then he turned.

"Luke, where are you going?"

He pointed. "I'll be over there with John, Jack and the other guys. You'll be safe in the tent with Elsie, Jess, Tina and the girls. See you in the morning, Love."

She watched as he walked over to where his sleeping bag was lying. Then she turned to go inside the tent. Elsie pointed to an empty sleeping bag and said she could change there in the tent if she needed to. Cathy wriggled out of her jeans to put on sweat pants, but she kept her sweat shirt. She folded the jeans and set them under the pillow for height. She got down into the bag and then zipped it up.

Once she had settled a few minutes had passed when she sat up. "Elsie," Cathy whispered, "what is that noise?"

"Noise?" Elsie sat up too.

"Yeah, that funny peeping sound."

"Oh, dear, it's just crickets. Go to sleep. They are outside. Don't worry."

"Crickets." Cathy repeated and lay back down.

The next day passed as quickly as the one before. When Luke had brought her back to her apartment, after waiting for the pictures to be developed, her spirit had been refreshed and renewed.

They had agreed that Luke would wait for Cathy to call him the next day. It was a holiday and no one was working. Cathy slept soundly and was surprised to see the time was after ten o'clock in the morning when she awoke. She rolled over and reached for the telephone.

Luke answered bright and cheerfully. "Good morning, Darlin'."

She laughed a little. "Luke, I haven't slept that well in a very long time. I suppose you've been up for hours."

"Just for a little while. I slept well too. What would you like to do today, Love?"

"Well, first I'm going to do my laundry. Then I think I'd like to go for a walk with you."

"Okay, when do you want me to come over?"

"Whenever you like. I'm going to take a shower now."

"I'll be there soon."

Cathy had hurried to put her clothes in the washer. No one

was out and about even though it was midmorning. Luke had parked in her parking space at her apartment building and came in while she was transferring her clothes to the dryer. She wasn't expecting anyone. When he greeted her using her pet name she jumped. When she turned to see who had spoken, she went to receive his embrace.

"I am so glad you are here. I think the laundry room is creepy now. You never know what to expect in here. All has been quiet though. Let's go back up stairs."

He stayed with her while she folded her clothes once they were finished drying. Once that chore was done and the clothes put away, they were on their way outside when Max hailed them from the office. The pleasant weather still held.

"Where are you two off to this nice day?"

"Oh, we're just going to walk in the park." Cathy told him.

Max commented. "Beautiful day for it."

They nodded and went out. They held hands as they strolled leisurely.

Finally Luke remembered something he was going to tell her. "By the way, Honey, Elsie's cat Missy is pregnant."

"Oh, that's nice." Cathy replied. Then she asked, "Does Jess know?"

Luke replied. "I think so. Seems Jess knows most everything before we do."

Cathy chuckled and nodded.

The afternoon passed quickly and peacefully. They were walking back when Cathy asked him.

"Do you want to take the short cut through the alley?"

"What do you think, Honey?"

"It's shorter. I don't mind as long as I am with you."

It had been quiet and peaceful in the park with few others there. Even traffic on the streets was light this day. Many people probably had gone out of town for the week end. Nothing was going to happen today Cathy thought to herself.

She was wrong.

They had walked a short distance down the alley when she saw it. Her grip tightened on Luke's hand and her eyes opened wide. She drew in her breath. Luke, too, seemed to stiffen. He glanced at her then back to the apparitional black figure ahead of them.

Luke released her hand and sprinted down the alley. The figure seemed to move sideways and disappear somewhere. When Luke reached the end of the alley he turned back but saw nothing. He stepped ahead to look around each side of the corners. Still no one could be seen. He turned and walked back to where Cathy was standing, still wide eyed.

"Luke, did you see it?"

He nodded.

She repeated. "You saw the cat person?"

He nodded again. "I saw the person dressed all in black and I saw the cat mask, but I don't know how it disappeared so quickly, or where it went."

Cathy sighed. "Finally. Now I am not the only one who has seen this thing. What can we do now, Luke?"

He sighed and said, "Write it down."

19. The Cat Stalker

Cathy tried to conduct her business as usual and not let her frustration get the better of her. She fought the fear that kept creeping into her being as the week progressed. When the phone rang on Wednesday afternoon she answered cheerfully. "Lein's Answering Line."

Then, the grated words drone forth in slow haunting rhyme.

Would that I could hold again
My precious Cat so feminine.
Why so frail, yet so fair?
Your loss leaves me in utter despair.

She dropped the receiver to the table with a clatter. Silence now surrounded her. Her breath came hard and fast. She began to pace around the living room. She was losing her battle with tears. What should she do? What could she do? She stared at the receiver still lying on the end table. Finally she reached out and picked it up. After replacing it in it's cradle she picked it up again and dialed the police station. When she got off the phone with the detective the time was close to 5:30 P.M. It would be too late to call Luke now.

In desperation she slowly bent down to a kneeling position on the floor. She bent her head onto the couch cushion and folded her hands to pray. When she stood, Cathy walked slowly to her bedroom to get her Bible. She looked up verses on temptation. When she found the one she had been looking for she reread it until she could recite it. Maybe this would help. She closed her Bible and glanced at her one window in the room. She went to hurriedly pull down the shade and closed the curtains. She had closed her eyes as she yanked the shade down. She didn't want to see anything, even if there was nothing there, she didn't want to look. She walked slowly to the kitchen to start a pot of coffee, reciting her verse as she went.

"'1 Corinthians 10:13. No temptation has overtaken you but such as is common to man; and God is faithful, who will not allow you to be tempted beyond what you are able, but with the temptation will provide the way of escape also, so that you will be able to endure it.'" After repeating it several times she prayed aloud. "Lord, please show me my way of escape."

The next time the phone rang it was a little after 9:30 that same evening. She experienced a torrent of emotions but had to make a quick decision or the answering machine would make it for her. She grabbed the receiver and put it near her ear. She merely said, "Yes?"

"Cathy, it's Luke. What's wrong?"

"Oh, thank God! Luke, it happened again. There was another horrid recording. I think you had already left the office for the day by that time and I just..."

Luke interrupted. "I'll be there in a few minutes." He hung up the phone.

Once he had called to her she unlocked the door for him. As he entered she repeated her biblical petition. Then she was surrounded by his warm strength in his tight embrace. Once she had calmed he asked her what the message said. She pointed to the bedroom where the answering machine sat stalwartly beside her bedside. They walked together into the room. She put on the overhead light and then replayed the tape for him. She turned and they walked back to the living room. Before he could ask any questions she spoke.

"I called the detective. He wasn't much help but he did say they might try to decipher where the call came from. Although, he doubted they could. He did think this was a threat though." She put her arms around him again for a comforting hug. She rested shakily in his embrace.

He kissed her gently several times. Finally he said, "I wish I could do something to stop this."

"Luke, your being with me is such a comfort. I am so very glad that you called."

"Do you want me to stay here tonight?"

Cathy looked up at him.

"I mean on your couch, just for safety. If anyone tries to come in..."

He could see by her expression that she hadn't anticipated this possibility. She merely said, "I don't know."

"Remember, Cat, you can trust me. I would never do anything to jeopardize what we have together. I know we must solve this awful situation before we can think seriously about us."

She made a small sound of surprise. "You, have been thinking seriously about us?"

He nodded.

She began to shake as sobs threatened again. "And, you would do that for me, stay here, on the couch?"

Again he nodded. His expression was sober but his eyes were wide with love.

She nodded and whispered her affirmation. Cathy secretly did not want to leave his supportive presence.

Luke gently shifted her weight pressing her forward slightly. He began to massage her tense shoulder muscles. He spoke soothingly. "You will never be able to sleep if you don't relax, Honey. Try to put it out of your mind."

Cathy was beginning to feel warm and prickly inside as tension lifted. With a sigh she came back to hug him and rested her cheek against his chest. His arms enfolded her securely as he silently prayed. They sat together on the couch, and fell asleep there.

In the morning, Luke had awakened first. His movement aroused her. She wanted to make breakfast for him before he left. Since she was so insistent about it, he asked if she would mind if he took a shower there. It would save time. She said he could while she prepared the bacon and eggs. Then she had pointed out, "Besides, we can pretend that we are already married." Her sweet smile quivered slightly. He had told her he could stop by his place to quickly change before going to work so he wouldn't look as if he had been sleeping in his clothes. She still wore her night clothes and robe which was still tigtly fastened around her. The night had been quiet with no other calls or interruptions.

He tried to hold a light conversation to help her mood, since Luke noticed Cathy seemed to relax a little while they ate.

Routine could have a calming effect on a stressful situation, Luke knew.

He told her, "The weather report is callin' for rain on Saturday and I am planning to go out on farm calls that morning. Are you on call this week end?"

She nodded.

"Well then, that worked out well this time. Hey, thanks for breakfast. This is great. I don't usually have but an English muffin or cereal and coffee myself."

"Actually, I don't even eat sometimes when I am alone, but I always make coffee." She told him truthfully. "See, you are good for me, Luke."

He had finished the last sip of his coffee and he rose to approach her. "Oh you are the best thing that has ever happened to me, Cathy. I mean it." His kiss was sweet and inviting.

She responded. They needed no words.

Then he said he had to go and she was to call him at any time if she needed him.

A couple of days later, on Friday, the police detective called to tell Cathy that they had not been able to determine a location for the calls she had been getting. She thanked him and hung up. This was no surprise. She felt that she would have to be resigned to fight her own battles by herself. At least she had the support of her man and her friends. This was comforting but she didn't want them to be in danger because of her. She wondered how, or if ever, this situation would come to a resolution. She tried to force herself not to dwell on that thought. She had more pleasant things to think about after all.

It was only minutes before noon on Saturday when Cathy called the veterinarian's office. Luke's receptionist answered.

"Dr. Hoffman isn't here right now. He's out on farm calls this morning."

Cathy asked quickly, "Do you know when he will be back?"

"No, not exactly, but he usually calls and checks in if he isn't coming back."

"Well, have you heard from him at all since he left?"

"No, he hasn't gotten back to us yet, Cathy."

Cathy sighed and then replied, "Please, please have him call as soon as you hear from him. I need to reach him."

"Well, I'm about to leave myself, but Miss Becker will be locking up today. I'll give her the message."

"Oh, no. That's not necessary." Cathy retorted with an edge to her voice. "I'll catch up with him later."

Cathy thanked her and hung up.

Rain was pattering against the windowpanes. The electricity had blinked off and then back on several times as she had to reset her microwave and stove clocks several times. Thunder rumbled restlessly it seemed and sometimes clapped impatiently. Cathy was on call this week end and couldn't leave. She just had to be patient and wait for her beau to return.

Luke had barely gotten into his car at the last farm call when the storm began to dump rain from the sky. He pulled his car around and drove out on the dirt road slowly. By the time he turned onto the main road the rain began to sheet across his windshield. He drove cautiously. It would be a long drive back to the city. He should have called the office or Cathy's apartment before he left, but he had wanted to get ahead of the impending storm. That tactic didn't work. At least he had seen all of his scheduled patients that morning and all was well with them.

When he came to his first intersection, Luke stopped for a long moment peering in both directions. He had seen no other traffic but he wanted to be sure nothing was coming before he turned out onto the straighter road that led back to the city. He could hardly hear the ticking of his turn signal as he rounded the corner. The rain seemed to drown out all other sounds and almost sights as well. Ahead of him the rear lights of another vehicle blurred through his watery view. Luke thought it had stopped for the rain also. He slowed, proceeding cautiously. He had not seen the black hooded figure, its driver, crouching on the road behind the other car. He hurled some small things onto the road behind his own car, then rose and hurried back to go inside it.

When he saw the other vehicle moving again, moving a little faster now, Luke continued ahead. Loud popping sounds, then Luke's car began to swerve and skid as if it had a mind of it's own. He fought to control it but the slick road would not yield to his efforts. The car spun and lurched sideways. Luke heard crashing, shattering sounds and then he heard nothing more as unconsciousness claimed him from his plunge over a small embankment and into a field. The other vehicle gathered speed as it move away quickly.

Cathy was wondering if she should call the police. It was not like Luke not to check in at the office. She didn't know his schedule for that morning and she was not about to call Lucy Becker to ask. She had spoken with Elsie who had informed her that Luke had already been there and gone. Elsie didn't ask him who else he was visiting that day. Cathy kept looking at her clocks. She would walk to the kitchen, then to her bedroom and back and forth. Finally she decided she had to do something. She sat on her bed and picked up the receiver. There was no sound. Well that explained why she had received no business calls that morning. The phone was dead...Luke...No she almost shouted to stop her mind from irrational thoughts. She sighed and put the receiver back in it's cradle. The phone was dead. Would the electricity be next?

Cathy did not hear the knocking at first. When it repeated, louder, she ran to the door, hurriedly unlocked and pulled it open. "Oh Luke!" She gasped.

"No ma'am. It's Max. I just wanted to check on you to see if you were alright. May I come in?"

"Oh. Well, I guess so. Sorry. I was expecting Luke." Cathy shut the door again. She gestured. "Sit down. Would you like some coffee?"

Max shook his head. "No, Cathy, but I would like to show you something. This is my scrap book." He pulled a binder out from his side. "This is very special to me, Cat."

She sat opposite him. Thunder boomed as she sat down. "Seems like a gothic novel." She murmured softly.

The man's gaze was intent upon her. "You know, you remind me of someone." He began.

She said nothing.

"You see, there was another Cat once." Max rose and came to sit next to her on the sofa. He took hold of her hands and held onto them tightly. "You are just like my Cat, my love, the one I lost over twenty years ago."

Her throat began to tighten. She tried to pull her hands away but his grip was too strong. She gasped when he began to wind a coarse rope around her wrists which he had pulled behind her back. "What are you doing?" Her voice was shrill.

"It's all in here, Cat. You see?" He opened the book and laid it on the coffee table. He was now tying a handkerchief around her head. It had gagged her mouth. She stared at the first page which held a newspaper clipping. The headline read:

Massabesic Lake Murder, Boyfriend Convicted

Inadvertently she leaned forward so that she could see the smaller print of the article. It told her that Cathleen Parker, age 18, had been raped and murdered by her lover while they were at the lake. The perpetrator, Frank Morrow, had been sentenced to 20 years in prison.

When he turned the page, she saw photographs of a younger Max with a young woman who could almost have been Cathy's double. There were some slight facial features and body mass differences, but the young woman resembled Cathy very closely, even to a similar style of glasses.

When Max turned the page again, two sonnets stared back at her. Max began to kiss her cheeks. Cathy pulled in her breath and tried to struggle. By now he had also bound her ankles. He turned the page again to reveal more sonnets. Max stood.

"I had to change my name after I got out. I tried to start over as Frank, but it didn't work out. When I saw you in Hanover, you looked so much like my Cat, still young, still beautiful. I got fired from that job at the recreation center when they found out who I was, so I moved and changed my name. When you came here I almost couldn't believe fate had brought us together again, Cat. Don't you see? It is meant to be, my love."

Her attempts at struggling were futile.

Max continued. "Don't worry about your boyfriend coming to your rescue. I had to get him out of the way, my Cat. He has had an accident."

Cathy could feel the color drain from her features. She felt suddenly chilled to the bone.

"Yes, you see, he wouldn't leave you alone. I saw the gifts he brought you and heard you talking with him and your other friends when you came in or left the building. The ironing board in the laundry room, those loose floor boards, the slashed tire, they were all meant for his benefit, as a warning. But he didn't heed it. He wouldn't leave you alone. So, I had to do it. It had to be, for us, Love."

Max reached for her, pulled her to her feet, then picked her up and laid her on the couch.

Through the ringing in his head Luke could hear sounds. Something was flashing as he blinked and opened his eyes. Something soft was under his head and he was lying on his back somewhere. "Cat." His voice was weak.

"Easy sir." A male voice spoke. "We are getting ready to put you in the ambulance to take you to the hospital. Just relax."

Luke swallowed and tried again. "Where's Cathy?"

The paramedic told him that he had been alone in the car.

Luke groaned then he spoke again. "Call Cathy."

"Who's Cathy?"

"Cathy Lein, my girl..."

"Okay," the paramedic interrupted him, "you want us to contact her for you?"

Luke tried to shake his head but the effort was too difficult. Luke's words came slowly as he mumbled them. "She might be in danger."

Thunder roared almost drowning out his plea. He swallowed hard again and repeated "Send police to Cathy Lein's apartment. She has a business, Lein's Answering Line. Hurry. She may be in danger. Please."

Luke choked. His throat was so dry.

"Okay, okay. Can you tell us your name?"

"Doctor Lucas Hoffman, DVM."

"All right, Dr. Hoffman. Don't worry about a thing."

The man hailed someone and a police officer appeared above Luke.

"Do you know anything about a Miss Cathy Lein?" The emergency service paramedic asked the officer.

The officer nodded and went to radio into the station.

"Cathy." Luke mumbled again.

"See. All taken care of." The male medic assured Luke. "Now you just rest." He motioned for help to lift the stretcher. "Let's get moving before we all catch pneumonia."

20. The Cat Stalker's Sonnets

Max turned his attention to his scrapbook again. He turned the page to reveal photographs of Cathy Lein, but she was unable to see it. She was lying on her back with wrists bound behind her and ankles tied together. Her mind was filled with scrambled thoughts. Fear and dread were tugging at her. She tried to think of Bible verses about fear but none came. Jesus had never been in this situation she thought. Then her mind spat back that Jesus had been bound much more painfully than she. He was made to hang with hands and feet nailed to wood. How He must have suffered. She felt little comfort in that at this moment, except that she was not alone in her plight. A verse emerged in her mind: "'Do not be afraid of them, for I am with you to deliver you,' declares the Lord." What book had that come from? Then another: "Trust in the Lord with all your heart and do not lean on your own understanding." Then she thought, Proverbs, chapter three.

Max had stepped back beside her. He was reciting some poem she did not recognize.

My love so strong, your love gone cold.
There is another Cat to behold.
I cannot quench this fire in my soul.
To another's arms I must go.

Then he began to kiss her tear stained cheeks again. When she tried to turn her face away, this seemed to anger him. She tried to utter a sound of fright as his body came down on top of hers, but it was just a muffle.

More Bible verses were emerging from her mind. Matthew 7:7. *Ask, and it will be given to you; seek, and you will find; knock, and it will be opened to you.*

She remembered another verse. *Behold, I stand at the door and knock; if anyone hears My voice and opens the door, I will come in to him and will dine with him, and he with Me.* (Revelation 3:20). The references were coming more readily now. All these faint voices were flooding into her thoughts in fleeting fractions of seconds.

Incredulously, at that moment, there came a knocking at her apartment door. Had she really heard knocking, or was it her sanity shattering? Then, a voice.

"Miss Cathy Lein?"

She tried to make some kind of sound as she wriggled, struggling against her assailant, but it was not loud enough to be heard.

Again the male voice announced, "Police, Miss Lein, open the door."

Max started to rise then. At the same time the door was opened. It was not locked. Two men wearing dark blue uniforms entered the room as Max headed for the bedroom and the fire escape. One man followed after him while the other went to untie Cathy. The scrapbook lay forgotten, open on the coffee table, waiting to reveal it's secrets.

The storm still raged outside reflective of the tumultuous events of that day. Once her bonds came off, Cathy began to blurt out her story to the officer.

Her words came fast, though hoarsely. She concluded with, "Max, that is, Frank, must have been the one who was stalking me. See, he had this notebook." She pointed to the object on the coffee table. She stepped over to look herself and her mouth opened wide as she stared at photos of herself. Her face must have paled too because the officer was asking if she was alright. She stammered, "I...I...had no idea."

The officer asked, "Have you ever seen this before?"

Cathy shook her head. She went back to sit down in a chair.

The officer pulled out a plastic bag from his pocket and some gloves in order to pick up the book. He also collected the ropes she had been tied with and her gag. Then he turned and said, "We'll be in touch, Miss Lein." He started toward the door.

"Wait." Cathy said. "What about...Max...Frank, the guy who was..."

He repeated. "We'll be in touch."

Cathy stood. "Officer, there is something else."

The man looked at her and waited.

"I haven't been able to reach my boyfriend, Dr. Lucas Hoffman. He's a veterinarian. He went out to make farm calls this morning and didn't check back in with his office. I was trying to get in touch with him, but I found that the phone was dead." She pulled in a breath then asked, "Did Max do that?"

The officer shrugged his shoulders. "We don't know yet.

Could have been the storm. I'll be right back." Without another word he went out.

Cathy sat waiting. Time seemed to hang over her like a thick blanket.

Only about 15 minutes had passed when the officer returned to report, but it had seemed like hours to Cathy.She felt the weight of fear as her heart pounded.

The officer told her, "Frank Morrow, alias Max Frazer, has been apprehended following a slight street chase. He is being arrested and is now handcuffed in the back seat of the squad car. Your boyfriend, Dr. Lucas Hoffman, has had an automobile accident and is being treated at Elliott Hospital."

She thanked him and he left.

Cathy locked her door and went to the phone praying that it would work. When she picked it up and heard a dial tone she immediately thanked God then called the Helpers. Next she called Luke's parents and gave them the hospital phone number. While waiting she also called Penny. Under the circumstances, Penny would be happy to cover for Cathy in order for her to take the following week as sort of an emergency vacation. Elsie and John both came to get her and take her to the hospital. She told them her story as they rode.

The doctor briefly explained Luke's condition to the three of them before they were allowed to go visit. Luke was just beginning to stir when Cathy leaned over him.

"Luke, Honey, it's Cathy. Can you hear me?"

He blinked and moaned. Finally he whispered her name.

"Easy, Luke," she told him, "you are in the hospital. You had an accident."

"Cathy, Darlin', are you all right?"

She nodded and smiled. She began to blink rapidly as tears of relief threatened to spill out. "Yes, my love, I am really all right now. I will explain later. The nightmare is truly over. How do you feel?"

He moaned again. After a few moments he spoke. "I thought you were in danger. I couldn't help. It was raining so hard and everything felt so heavy. My head hurts and my arms hurt."

She gently put her hands on his cheeks. "It's all right now, Sweetheart. Don't worry about anything. Just rest and everything will be all right. I promise."

"Cathy, I love you."

She gave him a gentle kiss and then released her hold. She repeated. "Just rest now. You will feel better soon."

Luke spent several days in the hospital with minor cuts, bruises, a sprained wrist and a concussion. Once released he was advised to take several more days rest before returning to work the following Monday. Cathy had insisted on taking the bus to tend to him during his recovery.

By the time Sunday had arrived, Luke insisted that he was well enough to attend church. Cathy had wanted to protest, but Luke was decisive about it. She had spent Friday and Saturday nights on his living room sofa. She marveled to herself that she was actually staying in a man's apartment at no risk to herself. However, her senses were acutely aware of his presence in the bedroom.

She had come a long way in being able to trust him. He had been instrumental in her life changing decision to put her complete and unguarded trust in the living Savior who was life blood to all who would believe in Him. Cathy thanked God for giving Luke to her.

Following service, everyone gathered at the Helpers' farm for Sunday dinner. The children had been sent outside to play before Cathy, with some encouragement, briefly retold her nightmare.

Elsie said, "Well, at least it is over for you now, dear. Thank God for that."

Next, John asked Luke to explain the events of his accident. Luke reported what the police had told him.

"I remember I had seen only one car during my trip back. It was ahead of me when I turned onto the main road heading back to the city. All I could see was a blur of the rear lights. It was raining so hard I could hardly see the road in front of me. I'll never forget that day. The police said it was Max...Frank, whatever his name is. Apparently he got out of his car and threw some nails in the road behind it. He must have waited for me to turn behind him. I blew a tire on those nails and lost control. The slippery road didn't help either. All I remember after that is asking for Cathy." He reached out to take her hand then continued. "They said I had a brief conversation with the paramedic but I don't remember it. When I woke up in the hospital the first thing I remember is this angelic face." He squeezed Cathy's hand.

Cathy added. "Max was the one writing those dreadful verses and playing those pranks on me. He kept a scrapbook and, I guess, confused his past with the present. From what I understand, he was in love with a girl named Cathleen Parker. According to the newspaper article that he kept, he raped and killed her."

"What happened to the scrapbook?" Jack Helper asked.

"The police have it." Cathy answered. Then she added,

"Those sonnets he wrote were a lament to his lost love. It must have been his way of dealing with it."

Then Luke commented. "But, he didn't deal with it very well if he went after you. By the way, I thought Max was right handed. I remember the detective told you the writing on the wall had been made by a left handed person."

Cathy answered him. "The detective learned that Max was ambidextrous. He could write with both hands although he used his right mainly. Oh, and the police got a search warrant. They found the black cat mask in his apartment along with the hooded sweat shirt and sweat pants which were all black." She sighed. "I guess he never recovered from the death of his first love. I just can't understand how he could have been so violent with her if he loved her so much." Cathy concluded. "He was the real black cat."

Jess spoke then. "Speaking of cats, where is Missy?"

Jack stood. "I'll go find her. Excuse me. I am finished. That was delicious, Ma."

Elsie nodded her thanks and smiled.

A few minutes later Jack reappeared. "Dr. Luke, your services are needed. Come to the attic. Missy has had her kittens."

Luke rose to follow Jack. When he returned he reported that mother and seven babies were all doing fine.

Elsie had called everyone back inside for dessert. The children all wanted to know when they could go and see once they had learned of the new arrivals. Elsie told them to give Mama some recuperative time, then they could start to visit the following day.

Then Elsie remarked. "It looks like there are enough so that

Cathy can have one."

Cathy gasped with surprise.

Elsie asked Luke, "Would it be all right if the three of us go with you to look, just briefly?"

Luke nodded. Elsie, john and Cathy followed him up stairs. Luke carefully picked up the female that looked most like her mama and handed it to Cathy.

"Oh, she is beautiful." Cathy exclaimed as she cuddled the small kitten. She looked up. "But I can't have a pet where I live."

"Well then," Luke began, "we'll just have to change where you live. Of course, if you are going to come live with me you'll have to change your name...to Hoffman."

Cathy opened her eyes wide, took in a breath, set the kitten back down on the floor by her mother and went to her man. "I think that would be...purr–fect. I love you, Luke Hoffman."

As they embraced John put his arm around Elsie's shoulders and began to lead her out of the small room. "Dessert's in the kitchen when you two are ready." He said as they walked out of the room together.

Following some kisses Luke spoke to her. "Now, about living with me, my apartment isn't very big and it doesn't have any land to speak of."

Cathy asked him. "What are you trying to say, Luke?"

"Well, John has already told me about their wedding gift to us. You know that piece of land where we went walkin' and ridin' by the pond?"

Cathy nodded, her eyes widened and her mouth opened.

"That's our wedding present. We can build on our new land."

"Oh, my, I just can't imagine it. I've never had a real home of my own. Oh, Luke, how wonderful!"

"Don't cry, Sweetheart." Then Luke said, "Cathy, Darlin', there is just one more thing. I know you said no gifts, but, if we are engaged to be married..." He pulled his arms back to dip into a pocket and brought out a small box. "I have to give you this."

She too pulled her arms free to take the object. She gasped when she opened it to find a sparkling ring. Luke picked it up, took the box from her to set it on an end table, then slid the ring onto her finger.

As they embraced her tears came freely. She threw her arms around his neck but held her hand up so she could gaze at her new engagement ring.

BONUS MATERIAL

The Sonnets

See the blind cat.
You can't escape that.
First to mate—
A fatal mistake.

Adult in body, but child in mind.
Reminiscent of innocence sublime.
Can't turn back the hands of time.
T'was truly frail, this feline.

Time's claws shred no memories.
Sickening pain haunts endlessly.
Again in vain I cry her name.
Each time silence fails to stop the pain.

Ne're to wed,
For now she is dead.

A time of innocence no longer mine.
I remember another frail feline,
A woman's body with adolescent mind.
Her fate sealed by providence divine.
Alas too late! They could not stop my love so blind.
Oh these ramblings of a shattered time.

 See the blind cat
Run for her life.
Though the blind cat
May escape once or twice,
Her sins find her out—
He knows her whereabouts.
Time to tame the shrew,
And now she is through.

The mind's a jackal so unkind.
From ramblings of a twisted mind,
Past and present make no difference.
A tragic waste of innocence.

Not that I loved too well or loved too much.
Would that again I could feel her touch.
Within my restless soul grows weary.
Why does love consume in fury?

Her short hair silky feline fur.
But that time I hugged she did not purr.
Her eyes shone dark as ocean depth.
My love, my Cat lay still as death.

Oh, Cat, my love, where have you gone?
In vain I'll search from dusk 'till dawn.

Would that I could hold again
My precious Cat so feminine.
Why so frail, yet so fair?
Your loss leaves me in utter despair.

Your skin so soft, your eyes so bright,
Burning, pleading in the night.
No one could compare to your beauty,
My precious and perfect Cathy.

My love so strong, your love gone cold.
There is another Cat to behold.
I cannot quench this fire in my soul.
To another's arms I must go.

How I long to feel your touch.
Oh my Cat, I miss you so much.

Jim's Sonnet

Roses are red,

Violets are blue,

A surprise is coming

From someone you knew.

Pretty Cathy don't you worry.

Put aside all anger and fury.

Not a doubt should remain.

No I am not your enemy.

Oh my timid lady so fair,

There is none who can compare,

To your incarnate beauty.

My love, there is none so rare.

Pretty lady there is no doubt,

You're the one I dream about.